have an impact—good or bad—on our minds, bodies, and spirits.

Poor feng shui can create problems—BIG pr~~oblems~~ especially i~~n~~ spirits can ~~b~~ start to sti~~

The most famous case study is a middle school in Missouri, where sixth-grade students had to use their beans to correct the school's feng shui.

REGARDING the SINK

REGARDING the SINK
Where, Oh Where, Did Waters Go?

KATE KLISE

Illustrated by M. SARAH KLISE

Gulliver Books
Harcourt, Inc.

Orlando   Austin   New York   San Diego   Toronto   London

Requests for permission to make copies of any part of the work
should be mailed to the following address: Permissions Department, Harcourt, Inc.,
6277 Sea Harbor Drive, Orlando, Florida 32887-6777.

www.HarcourtBooks.com

Gulliver Books is a trademark of Harcourt, Inc., registered in the
United States of America and/or other jurisdictions.

Library of Congress Cataloging-in-Publication Data
Klise, Kate.
Regarding the sink: where, oh where, did Waters go?/by Kate Klise;
illustrated by M. Sarah Klise.
p. cm.—(Regarding the—; 2)
Summary: A series of letters reveals the selection of the famous fountain designer,
Florence Waters, to design a new sink for the Geyser Creek Middle School cafeteria, her
subsequent disappearance, and the efforts of a class of sixth-graders to find her.
[1. Missing persons—Fiction. 2. Schools—Fiction. 3. Letters—Fiction.]
I. Klise, M. Sarah, ill. II. Title. III. Series.
PZ7.K684Reg 2004
[Fic]—dc22 2003026560
ISBN 0-15-205019-1

Designed by M. Sarah Klise with assistance from
Matthew Willis and Barry Age

First edition
A C E G H F D B

Printed in the United States of America

*Although the creators of this book do believe strongly in the principles
of* feng shui *and the power of beans, this is a work of fiction. All of the
characters and events portrayed in this book are the product of the author's
and the illustrator's imaginations. Any resemblance to any event or
actual person, living or dead, is unintended. No carp or cows or
fountain designers were harmed in the creation of this story.*

This book is dedicated to our nephew Sebastian von Zerneck, whose stock is *always* high in our book.

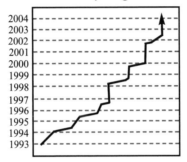

✑ **Annual Report** ✑

of the Sixth-Grade Class
at Geyser Creek Middle School

In which we describe
in chronological order
the significant activities
of the
academic year thus far,
including
(but not limited to):
feng shui
financial analysis
fraud detection
fund-raising
international travel
private investigation
search and rescue
and sink design

Of special interest to our shareholders is
our breathtaking (!) research into
cash flows
and
Waters,
Flo.

Geyser Creek Middle School
Geyser Creek, Missouri

September 7

Florence Waters
President and Boss
Flowing Waters Fountains, Etc.
Watertown, California

Dear Florence,

I hope you haven't forgotten about us here in Geyser Creek. We still talk about you all the time and think of you whenever we enjoy the fantastic fountain you designed for us.

Here's the funny thing, Florence. Now we need a new sink in the school cafeteria. Will you please help us design one?

Let me know, and I'll tell the others.

I miss you!

Your biggest fan and (I hope) best friend,

Minnie O.

P.S. Can you believe I'm in sixth grade? This year we get to take a class trip. Maybe we'll come visit you!

GEYSER CREEK MIDDLE SCHOOL
Geyser Creek, Missouri
Our school motto: "A Fountain of Youth"

Mr. Walter Russ
Principal

September 13

Ms. Florence Waters
President
Flowing Waters Fountains, Etc.
Watertown, California

Dear Ms. Waters:

Herewith a follow-up to my previous letter to you, dated September 6, in which I asked you to provide a cost analysis and design study for a new sink in the cafeteria.

The product we are seeking is described as follows in the *Middle-School Principal's Official Guide to Purchasing:*

Middle-School Principal's Official Guide to Purchasing

Chapter 22-A (a) 1.b-7 *Regarding Sinks*

A SINK is a basin-shaped receptacle connected with an outflow pipe leading to a drain or sewer. The purpose of a CAFETERIA SINK is to control liquid waste by first containing and then eliminating filthy and unnecessary waters.

It was certainly a pleasure working with you on the fountain. And I'll admit the underwater dictation station you installed is proving quite handy. (Thank you.)

But please be advised that the situation here in Geyser Creek is very different this year. Federal funding to schools has been cut by

90 percent, eliminating all extracurricular activities and nonessential staff.

Thus, we are even more committed than ever to staying on task, both academically and administratively. I have set many goals for Geyser Creek Middle School. I have no intention of letting myself, my staff, or our students become distracted by the installation of a new *sink*.

I'm confident we can accomplish this if we remember that a sink is simply a place where dirty and unnecessary waters go.

The bottom line then, Ms. Waters, is simply this: Let's not go overboard, okay?

Sincerely,

Walter

Walter Russ

☆THE GEYSER CREEK GAZETTE☆
Our motto: "We have a nose for news!"

Tuesday, September 21	50 cents

International News

Chinese Ship Sinks in Indian Ocean

A cargo ship sank in the Indian Ocean yesterday after an explosion ignited the vessel. No survivors have been found.

The SS *Sinkiang* was carrying cargo from China, including a container of mail bound for the United States and several containers registered to Growers of Alternate Sources of Power (GASP).

Authorities have not determined the cause of the explosion.

Rescue workers search for survivors from sunken ship.

Sen. Sue Ergass Visits Geyser Creek

Senator gives supporters her white-glove test

"Honey, where are we going with the hair?"

"Have a breath mint, Pops—now."

Sen. Sue Ergass visited Geyser Creek on a campaign stop yesterday. Ergass, an independent, is running for re-election to the U.S. Senate on a platform of More Opportunities for Missourians (MOM).

"Nobody cares about Missouri like your 'Senator MOM,'" Ergass told a crowd gathered at the Geyser Creek square. "Who's going to defend Missouri bean farmers like I did last year with my MO beans bill? 'Senator MOM,' that's who!"

Ergass used the campaign stop to explain why she supported cutting funding for schools by 90 percent.

"Kids today want everything given to them on a silver platter," Ergass said. "Well, tough beans! If they want a class trip, they can raise the money themselves. They want art lessons? Hire a teacher. It's time kids learned how the real world works. You want it? You pay for it. There's no such thing as a free lunch. Now stop

(Continued on page 2, column 2)

New Sink or Stink
Middle school needs new sink

On the heels of federal budget cuts that have slashed funding for class trips, school parties, art teachers, librarians, cooks, and custodians, the students at Geyser Creek Middle School have settled in for a "quiet, nononsense" academic year.

So said Principal Walter Russ yesterday in his first report of the academic year to the Geyser Creek School Board.

"The lack of distraction means we can focus on my major administrative goal, which is creating a letter-free school," Russ said. "Old-fashioned letters are an unnecessary burden for busy people like me. By March 1 all school correspondence will be sent electronically by BEAN-mail."

Brief Educational and/or Administrative Note correspondence, or BEAN-mail, is a free instant-messaging system developed for educational communication. All faculty and staff at Geyser Creek Middle School have been provided with a LIMA ('Lectronic Instant-Messaging Apparatus) for BEAN-mail use.

Principal Russ says school needs a new sink.

"This state-of-the-art technology will allow me to communicate with my staff anywhere in the world," explained Russ.

In other news Russ reported that even in these dire economic times, the cafeteria sink must be replaced because of a persistent clog.

"The sink is 40 percent clogged," Russ said. "Unless we replace the sink and its surrounding plumbing, we will have a serious problem controlling and eliminating filthy waters, which could create a real stink around here."

The school board established a sink replacement fund of $500. Russ is soliciting bids from various vendors, including Florence Waters of Watertown, Calif., designer of the school's unique fountain.

"There has been no response from Ms. Waters," said Russ, who did not seem entirely disappointed by the famous fountain designer's silence regarding the sink.

ERGASS *(Continued from page 1, column 2)* your bellyaching and line up so I can take a good look at you."

Ergass, known for her trademark white gloves, closed the rally as she did all of her campaign stops by enjoying a large bowl of pork and beans while offering free advice to her constituents.

In addition to serving in the Senate, Ergass writes the popular advice column "Because I Said So!"

Wall Street Wrap-up

Stocks to Watch	Yesterday's	Opening price:	Closing price:	Change:
	AIR-igate, Inc.	$18.49	$23.11	+25%
	Dyeing to Please	$1.56	$1.68	+8%
	Glum Gum	$1.78	$1.53	-14%
	Rainy-Day Rainwear	$1.22	$1.00	-18%
	Tough Beans	$1.22	$2.12	+74%

Mander and Eel Petition Denied

Judge Anne Chovey has denied Sally Mander and Dee Eel's request to submit a bid on the new sink for Geyser Creek Middle School.

Chovey, who popularized the "three scams and you're canned" sentencing guidelines, said at yesterday's hearing: "Mander and Eel have no business in sinks. Those two are where they belong—in the clink."

Mander and Eel were convicted in May after an investigation revealed their slimy business practices regarding the fountain in Geyser Creek Middle School.

Ima Crabbie Moves to Geyser Creek Senior Home

Leaving her home of 89 years was not difficult for Imogene "Ima" Crabbie.

"I might as well move," Crabbie crabbed yesterday. "I'm all alone in this big house with nobody to help me."

Mrs. Crabbie is the widow of Gus Russ and of Uri Crabbie. She has one child, Walter Russ.

Investor's Corner
By Macon Bigbucks, Investment Counselor

Remember, the secret to investing in the stock market is to buy low and sell high. You want to buy stocks at a relatively low price and then sell them when they increase in value.

Example: On Monday buy 500 shares of Rainy-Day Rainwear at $1 per share:

BUY price 500 x $1 = $500

On Tuesday Rainy-Day Rainwear stock rises to $9 per share:

SELL price 500 x $9 = $4,500

How to calculate profit:

$4,500	You sold for
- $500	You bought for
$4,000	**PROFIT!**

Ima going to move.

Trap Named Editor of Gazette

Annette Trap, longtime reporter for the *Geyser Creek Gazette*, was recently named editor of this newspaper. Ms. Trap will continue to report investigative stories.

"I love a good scoop," said Trap, who has a real nose for news.

Trap to serve as editor of *Gazette*.

When Budgets Are Lean, Kids Eat Beans

To save money Geyser Creek Middle School cooks have been dismissed. Prepackaged lunches will now be delivered to students on a conveyor belt. Meat, chicken, and fish dishes have been replaced by bean entrées.

No patty-melts on conveyor belt.

TODAY'S ASSIGNMENTS:

Math

- Need to discuss MONEY.
- How much will we need for a class trip?
- How can we raise it? Let's buy an ad in the <u>Gazette.</u>
- (And where are we going, by the way?)

Social Studies

- It's an election year. Let's compare the candidates.

Language Arts

- Decide on a good class MOTTO.*
- Write a letter to someone who embodies your motto. You may work together.

*WORD OF THE DAY: motto. a short sentence, brief phrase, or single word used to express a principle, goal, or ideal; a maxim

Here's one I like:
"A #2 pencil and a dream can take you anywhere." –Joyce A. Myers

GEYSER CREEK MIDDLE SCHOOL
SIXTH-GRADE CLASS
Geyser Creek, Missouri
Our class motto: "Adventure is worthwhile in itself." —Amelia Earhart

September 23

Florence Waters
Fountain Designer and Friend Extraordinaire
Flowing Waters Fountains, Etc.
Watertown, California

Hi, Florence!

Thanks again for all the cool stuff you sent us over the summer.
The wind chime sounds so pretty. (We hung it in the west win-
dow of our classroom, just like you suggested.) And the money
tree is growing like crazy. At first we thought real *money* might
grow on it. But then we did a little research and found out that
money trees *symbolize* wealth and prosperity, which is nice,
too. Thanks!

How are you? Are you off on another adventure somewhere?
Too bad we don't get to travel all around the world like you do.
We're going to take a class trip this year, but it'll probably just
be to somewhere boring, like a museum or a working farm.

So, Florence, are you really going to design a cafeteria sink for
us? We know fountains are your specialty. (You're only the most
famous fountain designer on the planet!) But we have no doubt
you could design a first-class, one-of-a-kind sink for us. (*Please?*)

Here are some ideas to get you started. ➜

THINK SINKS!

Here are my ideas:
- Put sink here.
- Instead of faucets, use hand-held devices.
- Glass wall and floor, so you can see where the stuff goes.

Tad Poll

Song of My Sink
By Minnie O.
A sink can be pretty, you know.
Its purpose is to help waters flow—
And direct them just so
The waters can go
Below to help flowers grow.
Florence, please make our sink beautiful, like the fountain.

SINK with built-in dishwasher and dryer

Other features:
* clothes washer/dryer
* pet washer/dryer
* body washer/aroma-therapy
* drive-thru service, for after recess and soccer games

Lily and Paddy

11

Build secret compartments in cafeteria table.

Gil

> Isn't it wonderful how all the children are eating their peas and beans this year?

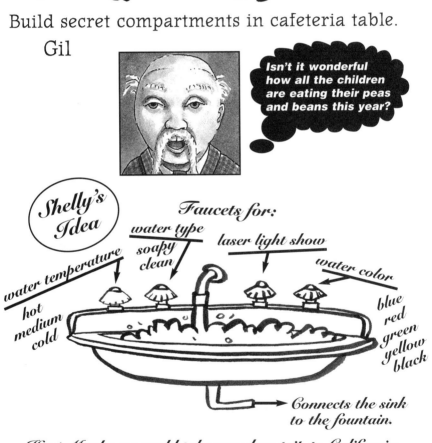

Shelly's Idea

Faucets for:

water type — soapy clean
water temperature — hot medium cold
laser light show
water color — blue red green yellow black

Dump gross food here.

Connects to sink. →

Connects the sink to the fountain.

Hey! Maybe we could take our class trip to California and help you build our sink. Let us know!

Sam N.
Sixth-Grade Teacher

Our class motto: "Adventure is worthwhile in itself." —Amelia Earhart

October 4

Florence Waters
Flowing Waters Fountains, Etc.
Watertown, California

Dear Florence,

Need I tell you how excited the students are about your possible return to our school? One word: *very.*

What they neglected to tell you is that the school board has created a sink fund to help *pay* for your sink-designing services. That is, if you're willing to take on this project.

I know you're extremely busy. Last we heard you were off to Sri Lanka to build a fountain. We'd love to hear about that. But then again, we love hearing anything from you.

When you have a moment, please let us know if you might be persuaded to design a sink for our school cafeteria.

Best regards,

Sam N.

P.S. I followed last year's fifth graders to sixth grade, so I'm responsible for organizing and chaperoning the fabled sixth-grade class trip. Naturally, this is the year all funding for class trips has been cut to $0. Speaking of sinks, I'm *sunk.*

✷THE GEYSER CREEK GAZETTE✷

Our motto: "We have a nose for news!"

Wednesday, November 3   **50 cents**

Sue Ergass Re-elected to U.S. Senate

Sen. Sue Ergass will represent Missouri in the U.S. Senate for six more years, thanks to her landslide victory yesterday.

In her acceptance speech Ergass promised a second term dedicated to protecting the rights of Missourians and serving as "everyone's MOM in Washington."

"Like a good mother I know what's best for you and I'm not afraid to tell you," Ergass told supporters at a victory party sponsored by the Growers of Alternate Sources of Power (GASP).

Ergass plans to continue writing her weekly advice column "Because I Said So!" (See p. 2)

Sen. Sue Ergass celebrates victory with supporters.

Ship Fumes Cause Fish Gloom

Authorities have not determined the cause of an explosion that sank the SS *Sinkiang* in September. Fumes from the burning wreckage are harming fish, aquaculturist Marina Byologee said yesterday.

"We're seeing widespread depression among the fish in a 250-mile radius of the *Sinkiang*," said Byologee.

All crew and passengers aboard the SS *Sinkiang* have been confirmed dead. Attempts are still under way to salvage remains of the sunken ship and its cargo.

Scientists link fish funk to area where ship sunk.

Because I Said So!

By U.S. Senator Sue Ergass

Dear Senator Sue:
What's with kids these days? They're not like they used to be. What's different about them?
Howie, Peculiar, MO

Dear Howie in Peculiar:

You're right. There's something different about this new generation.

Sure, they seem sweet enough. And they're certainly capable. There's no one on earth with more "can-do" spirit than a 12-year-old.

But wouldn't it be nice if children gave back once in a freakin' while? Wouldn't it be refreshing if they believed in something enough to WORK for it and make a little SACRIFICE instead of constantly grubbing for money for their self-serving class trips and low-rent school parties?

There are so many worthy causes out there. Why aren't children doing more to save the Sinkiang Blinking Spotted Suckerfish? It's a poor defenseless fish in China that will soon be extinct if someone doesn't take action.

Well, thank goodness "Senator MOM" is on the case!

Now, be good and eat your beans.

Why? Because I said so!

The Honorable Sue Ergass,
"Senator MOM"

More Opportunities for Missourians

Artist rendering of Sen. Ergass as a young public servant.

Investor's Corner

By Macon Bigbucks,
Investment Counselor

Do you own stock in AIR-igate, Inc.? If so, you made a wise investment. AIR-igate, Inc., the company that sells "new and improved rain," is forecasting quarterly profits of more than 225 percent.

The news came in a letter to stockholders from Snedley P. Silkscreen, founder and CEO of AIR-igate, Inc., and inventor of AIR-igation.

"People are tired of rainy days," Silkscreen said in his letter. "At AIR-igate, Inc., we eliminate pesky daytime rainstorms through carefully scheduled AIR-igation at night."

AIR-igation is currently available only in Europe and parts of Asia. The rain alternative is under review by the Stimulating Indigenous Natural Know-how (SINK) Committee in the U.S. Senate. If the technology is approved for use in the U.S., AIR-igate stock is expected to skyrocket.

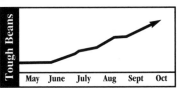

Federal funds fuel bean stocks.

Another stock to watch is Tough Beans, which has doubled in value in recent months based on investor confidence that bean sales will remain strong. Analysts point to the passage of the MO beans bill, which guarantees a serving of beans in every hot lunch served in elementary and middle schools. Sen. Sue Ergass (I-MO) sponsored the legislation.

Milk prices are on the rise overseas due to a decrease in milk production, while fuel prices are the lowest in history, thanks to an abundance of natural gas.

Dyeing to Please, producers of dyes for commercial use, rose 12 percent on bulk orders of permanent dyes.

BEAN-MAIL
Brief Educational and/or Administrative Note

```
To:    Mr. Sam N.
Fr:    Principal Walter Russ
Re:    Class trip
Date:  November 4
Time:  10:07 A.M.
```

I understand that the sixth graders plan to raise their own funds for a class trip. Please let me know: a) if this is true and b) where the students plan to go.

The sixth-grade class at Springfield Middle School just returned from a trip to Jefferson City, where they saw the Retired Librarians' Interpretive Dance Troupe's lively tribute to the Dewey decimal system. (See attached file.)

Also, Mr. N., can you try to keep your class a little quieter? Thank you.

Please respond by BEAN-mail.

Progressive Principal

This Week's Power Principal: Dulles Toast

Principal Dulles Toast of Springfield Middle School accompanied sixth graders on their recent class trip to Jefferson City. Toast freed up money in the school budget for a class trip by scrapping the school lunch program.

GEYSER CREEK MIDDLE SCHOOL
Geyser Creek, Missouri

Sam N.
Sixth-Grade Teacher

My motto: "I was a fantastic student until [age] ten,
and then my mind began to wander." —Grace Paley

November 4

Mr. Russ:

Yes, the students intend to raise funds for a class trip.

We're still discussing destinations. I'll let you know as soon
as the students decide where we'll be traveling. Like you,
they have set very high goals for this academic year.

I'm sorry for the noise. The students have been assembling
the build-your-own-beach kit that Florence sent them over
the summer. Don't worry. I disconnected the tidal wave
feature.

If you don't mind, I prefer my old-fashioned typewriter over
the new BEAN-mail system.

Sam N.

P.S. Do you think the Springfield students enjoyed the
Dewey decimal dance?

P.P.S. Are *you* planning to accompany *my* students on their
trip?

BEAN-MAIL
Brief Educational and/or Administrative Note

My motto: "Who said you should be happy? Do your work." —Colette

```
To:   Mr. Sam N.
Fr:   Walter Russ
Re:   Class trip
Date: November 5
Time: 9:22 A.M.
```

No and no.

But that's not the point. The bottom line is that a class trip must be educational in nature. See attached file from the *Middle-School Principal's Official Guide to Extracurricular Activities:*

▼

class trip: a supervised group excursion of an educational nature to a location off school campus for the purpose of firsthand observation

Let's not make this more complicated than it is.

A *beach* in the classroom? Highly unusual, Mr. N.

For all future Brief Educational and/or Administrative Notes, please use your BEAN-mail, Mr. N. That's what it's for.

November 8

Florence Waters
Boss and Owner
Flowing Waters Fountains, Etc.
Watertown, California

Dear Florence,

Just a quick note to say Hi!

We haven't heard from you in so long. Hope you're okay.

We're still raising money for our class trip. We're not sure where we're going. It depends on how much money we earn.

Last week we raised $14.25 by giving ice-skating lessons. This week we're delivering singing telegrams. Let us know if you'd like us to deliver one to you.

Of course, for you it would be free of charge!

Your friend,

Shelly

P.S. How's our sink coming along?

November 12

Ms. Florence Waters
Flowing Waters Fountains, Etc.
Watertown, California

Hey, Florence!

Are you mad at us? If we did something wrong, please let us know. We'd never do anything (on purpose) to offend you.

We don't have to come visit you in California. That was just an idea. We know you need your privacy.

Anyway, hope you haven't forgotten about us or our sink. We're still thinking of sinks and YOU here in Geyser Creek.

Your pal,

Gil

Could we do something like this for our new cafeteria sink? ▶──────────────────▶

The SMART Sink

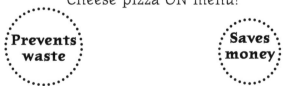

computer

Calculates uneaten food.

printer

Food goes in here.

scale

Monthly report: 327 pounds of beans down the drain

SMART Sink says: Beans OFF school lunch menu. Cheese pizza ON menu!

Prevents waste

Saves money

Please write back, Florence! We miss your funny letters and postcards. But mostly we miss *you*.

GEYSER CREEK MIDDLE SCHOOL
Geyser Creek, Missouri

From the Desk of Goldie Fisch

My motto: "A man has to be Joe McCarthy to be called ruthless.
All a woman has to do is put you on hold." —Marlo Thomas

November 15

Florence Waters
Flowing Waters Fountains, Etc.
Watertown, California

Dear Florence,

How are you? Busy, I'm sure.

I have a favor to ask. The sixth graders insist that you're the only person who can design a new sink for our cafeteria. They're hoping for something along the lines of the fountain you created for us.

(And have I told you lately what a *sweetheart* you are for including the aromatherapy whirlpool near the cattails on the east side of the fountain? So far I'm the only one who's discovered it!)

Back to business: I've tried to explain to the students that you're very busy with other jobs *and* that you might not even design sinks. But they'll hear nothing of it.

So, would you please send the kids a note, explaining that you'd like to help but have other commitments? I know they'll understand if they hear it from you. A letter from Florence Waters is always big news around here!

And for goodness' sake, don't feel you have to send the children any more gifts. We could open an exotic-animal petting zoo with all the glorious creatures you've sent us. One of the gibbons is sitting on my shoulder right now as I type. Oh! And two peacocks just sauntered into my office. (I've been feeding them candy corn. I hope that's okay!)

Florence, please take care of yourself. I'd hate to think the reason we haven't received a letter from you since summer is because you're ill. Even my boss, Principal Wally Russ (surely you remember *him*!), asked yesterday if we'd heard back from you regarding the sink. When I told him we hadn't, he said, "I hope nothing's happened to the old gal." *Old gal?* Oh brother.

Wally's big kick this year is getting rid of ALL "unnecessary letters." I wish he'd spend more time getting rid of the clog in the cafeteria sink. (It's really starting to smell.)

Meanwhile, the stink around town is that Wally's mother, Ima Crabbie, moved to the retirement home and Wally hasn't lifted a finger to help her settle in. You'd think a principal would treat his mother better, wouldn't you? I should write to Ima to see if she needs any help.

Now you know all the gossip. Did I forget to mention that your biggest fan and our best teacher is as adorable (and single) as ever? I'm talking about Sam N., of course. (Sigh.) I still chuckle to myself when I remember you telling me at Dry Creek Days that I should take a deep breath and ask Sam on a date. Florence, you just don't understand, do you? How could Sam N. ever be interested in boring old *me* when he can have a crush on the ever-mysterious and glamorous *you*? (Don't worry. I'm not jealous. Just realistic.)

Well, drop me a note and let me know you're okay, will you?

Your *concerned* friend,

Goldie Fisch

P.S. The enclosed devil's food cake is compliments of my sister, Angel. She said to apologize if it's dry, but milk is in short supply around here lately.

Geyser Creek Cafe
Angel Fisch, Owner

ANGEL'S DEVIL'S
FOOD CAKE

GEYSER CREEK MIDDLE SCHOOL
Geyser Creek, Missouri

From the Desk of Goldie Fisch

My motto: "A man has to be Joe McCarthy to be called ruthless.
All a woman has to do is put you on hold." —Marlo Thomas

November 16

Mrs. Imogene "Ima" Crabbie
Geyser Creek Senior Home
Old Pond Road
Geyser Creek, Missouri

Dear Mrs. Crabbie,

I read in the newspaper that you've recently moved to the senior home. My grandmother lived there for years and really liked it. Hope you will, too.

If you need any help settling in, may I suggest some able-bodied sixth graders? The students are trying to raise money for their class trip. I'm sure they'd be happy to do any chores for you at a very reasonable fee.

Happy (almost) Thanksgiving. Do you have plans to spend the holiday with family or friends?

Sincerely yours,

Goldie Fisch

Goldie Fisch
School Secretary

P.S. Your son, Walter, is my boss.

Geyser Creek Senior Home

Old Pond Road   *Geyser Creek, Missouri*

Imogene Crabbie

November 22

Miss Goldie Fisch
Geyser Creek Middle School
Geyser Creek, Missouri

Miss Fisch:

Let me tell you about your boss.

The man I USED to call my son lost nearly ALL MY MONEY for me. The fathead invested my life savings in one stock: Rainy-Day Rainwear. Who would buy stock in raincoats now that rainy days have practically been ELIMINATED?!

Luckily, I got out of the rainwear market before I lost everything. A year ago I invested my last $1,000 in AIR-igate, Inc., when it was trading at $4 a share. Well, you know what AIR-igate is, don't you? It's the new rain alternative that's sweeping Europe and Asia. The dadjing stock went through the roof, splitting four times and turning my 250 shares into 4,000 shares. Last I checked, AIR-igate was trading at $25 a share, meaning I've got a cool $100,000. Thank you, Snedley P. Silkscreen! Now THERE'S a man I'd be proud to call my son.

$1,000 Bought 250 shares @ $4/share
stock split = two for 1

So, I'm flush again. No thanks to your boss/my former son. I'd like to flush him down the toilet. I heard Wally still has all his money sunk in Rainy-Day Rainwear. He doesn't know BEANS about business. Imagine investing in raincoats!

1st split   500 shares
2nd split   1,000 shares
3rd split   2,000 shares
4th split   4,000 shares × $25
= $100,000

Well, I guess I don't need to tell you that if you work for him.

Now, about these sixth graders you mentioned. Lookit: I don't like kids (especially my own). And at 89 years old, I have no intention of changing. But I do need some work done around this dump. Have the rugrats come to the senior home on Friday at 4:00 P.M.

In case they're worried about working for Wally's mother, tell them I have nothing in common with that windbag.

And another thing: My name is MRS. IMOGENE CRABBIE. If any of those pip-squeaks call me Ima (as some people in this crummy town do), IMA likely to twist their noses off with my fingers.

That's all.

Imogene Crabbie

Imogene Crabbie

P.S. What's with this MOTTO business? Do you want to know my motto? Here it is: "I'll give you something to cry about."

P.P.S. Thanksgiving? Bah.

FLORENCE,

This is the time of year

we give thanks

for all of life's blessings,

ESPECIALLY
~~including~~ friends like you.

Happy Thanksgiving!

Gil

Here's another idea for the sink!

leftover beans—ugh!

The Bottomless Sink
for all the dirty
lunch dishes

Florence,
We know you're busy. Just want to say we're thinking of you at this time of year—and always.
Love,
Lily and Paddy

We all miss you, Florence! (Especially me.) Please write back.
Minnie O.

If you ever need a singing telegram, holler!

Shelly and Tad

Florence:
Please let us know your thoughts on our possible class trip to California. Are you available for a visit? If not, we'll take a rain check.
—Sam N.

P.S. I sincerely hope we didn't offend you by asking for your help with the sink. No hard feelings?

December 7
HOT-LUNCH MENU: frank & beans

TODAY'S ASSIGNMENTS:

Language Arts
	Write a story, essay, poem, or letter regarding a sink.
	Use any of its many meanings.

WORD OF THE DAY: sink 1. a basin connected to a
supply of water at one end and a drainpipe at the other.
2. to move to a lower level 3. to appear to move or to
slope downward 4. to become weaker, quieter, or less
forceful 5. to diminish, as in value 6. to decline, as in
morale 7. to seep 8. to make an impression or become
understood (usually with in)

Usage: Is it sinking in how much money we'll need to
raise if we want to visit Florence in California?

If I Were A Sink
By Minnie O.

You can think of a sink
as the place where water flows.
You can think of a sink
as the hole where stinky food goes.

You can think of a sink
while you watch the grass grow.
You can think of a sink
till all the roosters crow.

But the more that I think
about thinking about sinks,
the more that I think
I wish I were a sink.

Because if I were a sink,
then maybe I'd know:
Where, oh where, in the world
did Florence Waters go?

EXCELLENT! This is terrific, Minnie! Please work with Shelly
and set it to music. I'll buy it as a singing telegram for Goldie.

Mr. N.

32

THE FISH

December 20

Florence,
Warm wishes for
a wonderful
holiday season!
Peace* on Earth

From your friends in Geyser Creek!
Lily   Paddy   Tad Poll

*And peas and beans down the sink!
Remember that idea I sent you regarding
the sink? You can use it if you want to.

Merry Christmas, Florence!   Gil

FUNd-raising is no FUN?
In four months we've raised
only $79.03. So don't worry,
Florence. We'll never be able
to afford a class trip to California. We'll probably just go
to Springfield. (Snore . . .)
                          Shelly

Florence:
You don't have to write back
if you don't want to. No matter what,
I'll never forget you.   Minnie O.

Florence,
We won't bother you again.
                          Sam N.

A. V. Aytor

January 3

Mr. Sam N.'s Sixth-Grade Class
Geyser Creek Middle School
Geyser Creek, Missouri

Dear Sixth-Grade Class:

I must begin by asking for your forgiveness.

I'm Florence Waters's personal pilot. And I'm ashamed to say I read the letters you sent to Florence.

I know that reading other people's mail is a federal crime. (As it should be!) But I also know that Florence left on a trip in September. She didn't say where she was going. She didn't even arrange to have her mail forwarded, as she usually does. She just said she had some important research to do and that she'd be back soon.

But that was four months ago. I haven't seen her or heard a word from her since.

When your letters began arriving in the fall, I was filled with hope. Florence told me what a wonderful time she had with you all. I saw the Geyser Creek postmarks and thought: *Well, of course! Florence went back to Geyser Creek to spend time with her friends.*

Then the weeks wore on, and your letters continued to arrive. But still, no sign of Florence. Finally, this morning I opened your letters—only to learn that you haven't heard from her, either.

Please forgive me for reading your letters. I only hoped to find out that Florence is all right. Now I'm more worried than ever.

If you hear from Florence, will you please let me know? She's my dearest friend in the world.

Sincerely,

A. V.

Ariel Veronica Aytor

P.S. Hope you found someone else to help with your sink. Florence had just begun sketching ideas when she left on her research trip. (See attached pages from her sketch pad.)

Various Ideas regarding the Sink

Winking Sink

Eye-inspired sink uses a "wink" to flush food down sink.

Pedestal Sink

Teeter-totter balances hot/cold water.

Drinking Sink

Sink washes dishes by "drinking" them.

Rink Sink

Ice Sculpture

Breakdown of food + digestive enzymes generates heat and allows food to pass through sink without melting ice.

* Must eliminate the clog. Stagnant waters are worse than no water at all.

GEYSER CREEK MIDDLE SCHOOL
SIXTH-GRADE CLASS
Geyser Creek, Missouri
Our NEW class motto: "One of the oldest human needs is having someone to wonder where you are when you don't come home at night." —Margaret Mead

January 6

Ms. A. V. Aytor
c/o Flowing Waters Fountains, Etc.
Watertown, California

Dear Ms. Aytor,

Thanks SO much for your letter. We're halfway relieved because now we know Florence isn't mad at us. But like you, we're also worried half to death.

Don't worry, Ms. Aytor. We'll find Florence. She helped us last year. Maybe it's our turn to help *her*. Besides, as Florence might've told you, we're *awesome* private investigators!

Yours in search of Waters,

Lily   Tad   Minnie O.   Gil

Paddy   Shelly

P.S. We know Florence would understand why you opened our letters. Florence's mail might provide the only clues that can help us find her. Who else has been writing to her lately?

P.P.S. Any friend of Florence's is a friend of ours! —Sam N.

A. V. Aytor

January 14

Mr. Sam N.'s Sixth-Grade Class
Geyser Creek Middle School
Geyser Creek, Missouri

Dear Lily, Paddy, Gil, Tad, Shelly, and Minnie:

I've spent all week opening Florence's mail. Phew! Here's what I can report.

In the past four months Florence has received:

- 429 requests for fountain designs (including one from the queen of England)

- 645 postcards from friends all over the world

- 11 marriage proposals (a cliff diver in Mexico asked eight times!)

- 826 magazines and periodicals, including the *Congressional Record*, which Florence reads cover to cover

- Something that looks like a meteor fragment, but the label says it's devil's food cake

- 217 bills that I'd better start paying before—

Ack! There goes the electricity. I hope this information is enlightening. I'm still in the dark—in more ways than one.

Please write if you hear anything about Florence.

Sincerely,

A. V.

Ariel Veronica Aytor

P.S. to Sam: I feel like I know you already after all Florence told me about you. If it's any comfort, she had this note taped to the hallway mirror:

Must get priceless gold for Sam.

✫ THE GEYSER CREEK GAZETTE ✫

Our motto: "We have a nose for news!"

Wednesday, January 19   **50 cents**

Sixth Graders Turn On Fund-raising Efforts Full Blast

Sixth-grade students at Geyser Creek Middle School held a press conference yesterday to announce more than a dozen new services they're offering to raise funds for their class trip. (See special advertising insert in today's paper.)

"We're really motivated to raise money because it's no longer a simple class trip," explained Tad Poll. "It's a matter of life or death."

Poll refused to say where the sixth graders will travel. When pressed he said simply: "Let's just say we're going to go with the flow. But we think it'll be a blast."

Snow-shoveling special nets $17.50 for the sixth-grade class-trip fund.

Principal Calls Sink Stink "an Opportunity for Dialogue"

In his monthly report to the school board yesterday, Geyser Creek Middle School Principal Walter Russ said the unpleasant odor in the cafeteria is due to the sink, which is now 60 percent clogged. Russ said he has not chosen a replacement sink.

"I'm considering various bids," reported Russ, who is overseeing the $500 sink fund. He said he has not received a proposal from Florence Waters of Flowing Waters Fountains, Etc.

"I think someone right here in Geyser Creek could design a sink for us," Russ said. "I see this sink clog as an opportunity for dialogue. I invite everyone in Geyser Creek to send me ideas for the new sink."

Hairstylist Pearl O. Ster suggested a self-shampooing pink sink.

"I propose a pink sink that students can use to wash and style their hair between classes," said Ster, who wore a decorative gas mask to the meeting. "The sink stink makes me dizzy," she explained.

In other news Russ said he is enjoying the new BEAN-mail system and is encouraging his staff to use a LIMA ('Lectronic Instant-Messaging Apparatus) for all Brief Educational

Hairstylist Pearl O. Ster proposes a pink sink.

and/or Administrative Notes.

"With BEAN-mail we can eliminate old-fashioned letters from school," said Russ, who continues to purge his office of all unnecessary letters.

Because I Said So!

By U.S. Senator Sue Ergass

Dear Senator Sue:
I've never heard of the Sinkiang Blinking Spotted Suckerfish. Is it really almost extinct? Gosh! What can I do to help?
Mimi, St. Louis, MO

Dear Mimi in St. Louis:
Were you paying attention in school? If so, you would know that the Sinkiang Blinking Spotted Suckerfish is a rare species found only in China. It has bright red spots on its gills and blinks repeatedly when it's happy.

The problem is this lovable fish is being flat *fished out* by the Chinese people. Why? Because they don't have another reliable source of protein!

Thanks to my MO beans bill, more than 200 million pounds of Missouri beans have been sent to China. But it's not enough. They need more beans!

That's why I'm calling for a massive, door-to-door bean drive to collect canned beans for the people of China. That way they can eat the beans and save the fish.

I'm calling it the BLAST! drive because Beans Lift America's Spirit Tremendously!

Now, be good and go get me some beans. Why? Because I said so!

The Honorable Sue Ergass,
"Senator MOM"

More Opportunities for Missourians

Geyser Creek Cafe

Chocolate milk: now $2 a glass
Sorry, folks! Milk prices are out of this world!

Angel Fisch, Owner

AIR-igate Stock Still Hot; Raincoat Sales a Wash

Profits continue to rise at AIR-igate, Inc., which posted record gains this week. Investors speculate the biggest profits will come when the new "rain alternative" is approved for use in the U.S.

The Stimulating Indigenous Natural Know-how (SINK) Committee in the U.S. Senate held hearings this week on the safety of AIR-igation. Environmentalists contend the fake rain has an odd smell.

"It's 100 percent natural," insisted AIR-igate, Inc., founder and CEO Snedley P. Silkscreen, who testified by videophone.

Silkscreen was invited to appear in person before the Senate panel but chose to testify from his branch office in China. Sources close to Silkscreen say the former dairy farmer shuns public appearances and has an obsession with cleanliness.

"Snedley's scared to death of germs," said one source. "He wears a gas mask to protect himself from airborne bacteria."

Rainy-Day Rainwear investors can now wear free raincoats. This week Rainy-Day Rainwear, which is teetering on the verge of bankruptcy, sent complimentary raincoats to its major investors.

"It's our way of thanking investors for weathering this financial storm with us," said Rainy-Day Rainwear CEO Mel N. Collie. "Besides, with AIR-igation on its way out, nobody else wants this stuff."

Collie acknowledged that AIR-igation has eliminated the need for raincoats in much of the world, causing stock in his rainwear company to plummet.

"Basically, we're sinking like a lead balloon," he said.

Meanwhile, worldwide milk production is down sharply, leading to higher prices and leaving a sour taste in the mouths of consumers. Analysts have indicated the decrease in milk production is linked to Missouri dairy farmers who are abandoning dairy operations and converting their farms into bean fields to benefit from federal bean subsidies.

Wall Street Wrap-up

Stocks to Watch	Yesterday's	Opening price:	Closing price:	Change:
	AIR-igate, Inc.	$47.23	$93.51	+98%
	Dyeing to Please	$2.96	$3.37	+14%
	Glum Gum	$1.98	$1.50	-24%
	Rainy-Day Rainwear	$ .50	$ .27	-46%
	Tough Beans	$4.27	$5.12	+20%

Ima Crabbie Buys Senior Home

Using carp, kids to "clean up this dump"

Ima Crabbie moved into the Geyser Creek Senior Home in September. Now she's bought it.

Crabbie plans to revive the old pond behind the retirement community.

"I've ordered a couple of Chinese grass carp to eat off all that old pond scum," Crabbie said yesterday. "And I hired some of those rugrats over at the middle school to help me clean up this dump. Why not? My AIR-igate stock has gone through the roof and I've made a bundle. Might as well spend it. I don't have anybody to leave my money to."

Crabbie uses grass carp and kids to clean up senior home.

Investor's Corner

By Macon Bigbucks, Investment Counselor

What feeds the stock market? A lot of things, including fear and greed. But pay close attention to supply and demand. When consumer goods are in short supply and high demand, prices rise. When demand is low but supply is high, prices drop.

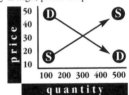

A Public Service Message from "Senator MOM"

Senate Bean Soup

Did you know that bean soup is on the menu every day in the U.S. Senate restaurant? It's true! Now you can make it at home.

The Famous Senate Restaurant Bean Soup

2	pounds dried navy beans
4	quarts hot water
1½	pounds smoked ham hocks
1	onion, chopped
2	tablespoons butter
	salt and pepper to taste

Wash the navy beans and run hot water through them until they are slightly whitened. Place beans in pot with hot water. Add ham hocks and simmer approximately three hours in a covered pot, stirring occasionally. Remove ham hocks and set aside to cool. Dice meat and return to soup. Lightly brown the onion in butter. Add to soup. Before serving, bring to a boil and season with salt and pepper. Serves 8.

www.senate.gov

AT YOUR SERVICE!
The SIXTH-GRADE Class Can HELP YOU!

Private Investigations
Contact Paddy

Singing Telegrams—the Perfect Gift!
Call Shelly

Pet Services,
Walking and/or Washing
Talk to Tad

Tours of the Fountain and
Ice-skating Lessons
Meet Minnie

We put the FUN back in FUNd-raising!

Let us fix your lunch!
Call Lily
"I've been packing my own lunches since 1st grade."

Photography
Get Gil
"I've got a dark room!"

Private Concerts in Your
Home or Office
Sam N.'s Tune-A Combo

Call us to:
- Shovel your driveway
- Paint your kitchen
- Entertain at your next party
- Write an original poem or song for you

This week's special: We'll solve your math problems! No problem too small.

DON'T FORGET: It's for a GOOD CAUSE!

All money raised will be used for our CLASS TRIP.

TESTIMONIAL:
"Lookit, these pip-squeaks do pretty good work. Plus, they're dirt cheap. That's all."
— Imogene Crabbie

GEYSER CREEK MIDDLE SCHOOL
Geyser Creek, Missouri

Mr. Walter Russ
Principal

My motto: "I'd rather be using BEAN-mail." —Walter Russ

January 19

Mrs. Imogene Crabbie
Geyser Creek Senior Home
Old Pond Road
Geyser Creek, Missouri

Dear Mom,

Because you refuse to see me or accept my phone calls, I am forced to write a letter to you, which is something I've been trying to cut back on.

It has come to my attention that you have hired some middle school students to do odd jobs. This is very generous of you. (Some might say unusually so.) However, please be advised that I am willing to perform any chore for you free of charge.

I apologize for investing your money in Rainy-Day Rainwear. I thought rainwear was a safe investment. Apparently, I was wrong. But I'm still your only child.

All of which is simply to say: If you need anything (big or small) done around the senior home, please call me rather than the children. I would like to help you.

Very truly yours,

Walter

Walter "Your Only Son" Russ

44

Geyser Creek Senior Home

Old Pond Road   *Geyser Creek, Missouri*

My motto: "I'll give you something to cry about." —Imogene Crabbie

January 21

Walter Russ
Overpaid Bean Counter
Geyser Creek Middle School
Geyser Creek, Missouri

Wally:

HELP me? I've had enough of your *help.*

Losing almost my ENTIRE LIFE SAVINGS was bad enough. But now you think you can tell me how to spend the money I made in the stock market? Why? Do you think you're going to inherit any of it? WRONG!

If I want to hire the pip-squeaks from the middle school, I will. Don't call me *Mom.* And don't contact me again. EVER!

Imogene (that's "Mrs." to you) Crabbie

Here's my idea for your new sink. I call it the FINK Sink because anytime YOU walk by, it nails you with a good squirt in the eye!

45

BEAN-MAIL
Brief Educational and/or Administrative Note

My motto: "No good deed goes unpunished." —Clare Booth Luce

```
To:   Mr. Sam N.
Fr:   Principal Walter Russ
Re:   Class trip and bean drive
Date: January 24
Time: 8:42 A.M.
```

Have you decided where you're taking the sixth graders on their class trip? Please advise asap via BEAN-mail. (Use your LIMA, Mr. N.)

This week's edition of *Progressive Principal* mentions a traveling museum exhibit that chronicles the history of Silent E. Perhaps we could arrange for the show to come to Geyser Creek, thereby eliminating the need for travel outside city limits.

Also, please urge your students to bring in canned beans for the bean drive. The sixth graders at Springfield Middle School have already collected 500 cans.

See attached files. ▼

Progressive Principal

Traveling Museum Exhibit

In this dramatic show, a talented mime reenacts the fascinating history of Silent E, "The Shy Star of the English Language."

Toast with Beans

Principal Dulles Toast of Springfield Middle School agreed to eat a can of cold garbanzo beans if his students brought in 500 cans of beans.

46

Sam N.
Sixth-Grade Teacher

My motto: *I hear and I forget. I see and I remember. I do and I understand.*
—*Chinese proverb*

January 25

Mr. Russ:

As long as typewriters are still legal, I'd like to continue using mine to write letters, rather than using a LIMA to send BEAN-mail.

The class trip is still under discussion, sir. I will advise you of the destination as soon as the students decide.

Sam N.

P.S. Do you think my class would *enjoy* the Silent E show?

P.P.S. Are *you* willing to eat a can of cold garbanzo beans if my students bring in 500 cans of beans?

BEAN-MAIL
Brief Educational and/or Administrative Note

My motto: "We are not amused." —Queen Victoria

To: Mr. Sam N.
Fr: Principal Walter Russ
Re: Class trip
Date: January 25
Time: 11:07 A.M.

No and no.

But that's not the point. It's the *principle* of the thing.

I have an office full of Rainy-Day Rainwear that your students may have if they agree to bring in 600 cans of beans.

You may also have a letter that I received a few months ago from your friend Florence Waters. (I'll put it in your NONelectronic mailbox.)

I certainly don't need the letter, and I don't want it cluttering up my (almost) letter-free office. It is my experience that nothing good ever comes from sending or receiving letters.

'FLOWING WATERS FOUNTAINS, ETC.'

Watertown, California

September 16

Wally Russ
Princey Pal
Geyser Creek Middle School
Geyser Creek, Missouri

Dear Wally Russ,

So you need a new sink for your cafeteria, do you?

I'd be tickled to help. But I should tell you something: I've never designed a sink before. Splendiferous fountains with OTT (that stands for Over The Top) features are my specialty.

So just give me a little time—and *please* don't ask how much—to do some research on sinks. And can we please remember not to call my research "gallivanting" this time?

Wally, I'm worried about your *feng shui*. Do you have a turtle? They're excellent for activating good *feng shui*. Also, I know how you resist physical activity, but please practice the following exercise. You can do it while sitting at your desk or standing.

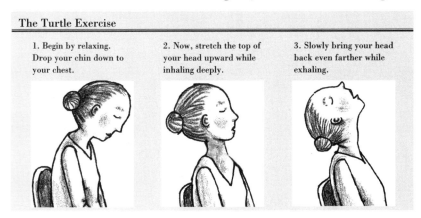

The Turtle Exercise

1. Begin by relaxing. Drop your chin down to your chest.

2. Now, stretch the top of your head upward while inhaling deeply.

3. Slowly bring your head back even farther while exhaling.

Repeat eight times daily. (Yes, EIGHT times daily, Wally! Please.)

Now, Wally, don't get mad at me for giving you these assignments. I do it only because I care about you. Why? Because you're a peach! Don't you dare listen to people who say you're the pits. I know who you really are. You're my cutie-patootie, Wally Russ!

But we must do something about that sink. There's nothing more damaging to the *feng shui* of a school than a body of stagnant water. It can turn the precious *chi* stale and harm all who work near it.

Gotta dash. My ship sails for Sinkiang later tonight. I'm traveling cargo class for a change—FUN!

Cheers!

Florence Waters

P.S. I can hear you blushing from here. Relaaaaaaaaaax, Wally! I have no designs on you—other than sink designs.

wall-mounted sink

Wally-mounted sink!

P.P.S. What was that hoo-ha in your letter about a sink being a place where "dirty and unnecessary Waters go"? Pooey! If you're referring to someone in my family, you'll have to be more specific. Even then, I refuse to take your insults to heart, Wally. Why? Because I like you! So there. Put *that* in your snorkel, you lovable dictator you!

P.P.P.S. Do you really think that you can contain and eliminate Waters with a sink? Here's the real bottom line:

It's a good thing you're still in school, Wally, because you've got a LOT to learn.

January 26
HOT-LUNCH MENU: soybean burgers

TODAY'S ASSIGNMENTS:

We have some clues about Florence!

Need to research SINKIANG.
Where is it? Why did Florence go there?
You may work together.

- Use reference books.
- Post all info on bulletin board.

Everyone please thank Principal Russ for sharing his
letter from Florence with us. (And for the raincoats, too.
Anybody want one?)

WORDS OF THE DAY: feng shui. Please look up the term.

SINKIANG: Sinkiang Uighur (also spelled Xinjiang Uygur) is in China!

Why Might Florence Travel to Sinkiang, China?
By Tad and Lily

We think Florence went to Sinkiang to do research for our sink. (It is SINKiang, after all.) Or maybe she fell in love with someone in Sinkiang. Maybe she got married to the cliff diver!
   Sorry so short. We've gotta run over to the senior home. Mrs. Crabbie has more work for us.

Feng shui (pronounced fung shway) is the 4,000-year-old Chinese art that promotes happiness and health. It's the belief that you can live in harmony with your environment so that the energy surrounding you works for you rather than against you. —Paddy

Feng Shui = The Art of Flow
Some people call *feng shui* the art of flow because the goal is to harness the flow of positive energy, called *chi*. You have good *feng shui* when the winds and waters surrounding you are harmonious and well balanced. —*Shelly* and Gil

Sinkiang, China
By Minnie O.
   Sinkiang has rugged mountains and vast desert basins. Life is not easy for the people who live there. Most are farmers who spend their lives wandering the dry plains, looking for pastureland to graze their animals.
   The climate is very dry, so irrigation is extremely important. Irrigation means using ditches, pipes, or streams to bring water to dry land. Almost 90 percent of the cultivated land in Sinkiang relies on irrigation.

EXCELLENT RESEARCH!
Let's not forget our fund-raising efforts. Do we want to auction off Florence's letter? Let me know your thoughts.

Mr. N.

10 Reasons Why We Should <u>NOT</u> Auction Off Florence's Letter to Wally

By Tad and Lily

1. Because it's our best clue about where Florence is.

2. Because we need it for our research.

3. Because it's pretty.

4. Because it might be even *more* valuable some day.

5. Because it's a letter from Florence, for pete's sake!

6. Because it's not legally ours, is it? (Isn't it Wally's?)

7. (Alternate position) Because if it *is* ours, we should treasure it.

8. Because some of us just don't want to sell it, dang it.

9. Because this might be the last letter we have to remember Florence by.

10. Because there are other ways to raise money for our class trip.

Instead of auctioning off Florence's letter, what if we invest the money we've raised so far in the stock market? It's risky, but maybe we could double or triple or QUADRUPLE our money. We'd like to interview Mrs. Crabbie and find out how she made so much money in the stock market.

Sounds good. Let's hear your report tomorrow.
Mr. N.

How to Make Money in the Stock Market

By **Tad** and Lily

Our source for this report was Mrs. Imogene Crabbie, who has made a ton of money in the stock market.

More than $400,000, to be exact. We began our interview by asking Mrs. Crabbie if she would share her best tips for choosing winning stocks.

Her answer was, "It's easy. You just have to use your bean and follow your nose."

Mrs. Crabbie said it's important to sniff around for bargains. She also said you should find out everything you can about a company before you invest in it. The best information can be found in a company's annual report.

We thought once you got out of school, you wouldn't have to write reports. But it turns out if you want to go into almost any business, you still have to write reports.

And if you want to invest in the stock market, you have to read reports. If you're thinking about buying stock in a company, it's a good idea to call or write and ask the company to send you its annual report. Or you can look for the company's annual report online.

Or you can just ask Mrs. Crabbie. She's got a zillion annual reports in her apartment, like this one from AIR-igate, Inc.

Mrs. Crabbie says it's her favorite stock. It's so good, she invested ALL of her money in AIR-igate. Maybe we should invest our class-trip money in AIR-igate, too.

AIR-IGATE, INC.

ANNUAL REPORT

The modern alternative to RAIN . . .

Because by improving on Mother Nature, we all GAIN.

Why let rain ruin your plans?

Stop **WAITING.**

Start **AIR-IGATING!**

With AIR-igation, rain is delivered at night—so you can enjoy your days!

"It's like rain, only better!"

precision targets

some casualties unavoidable

Sorry!

low financing	47.3% interest rates	rent-to-own water

AIR-igate was named #1 by a U.S. senator dedicated to improving nature.

Senator Sue Ergass (MO)
Our friend in Congress!

AIR-IGATE, INC., CORPORATE MOTTO: "Flowing waters are nice, but cash flows are nicer."

Greetings, investors! Let's have a look at the numbers.

**Snedley P. Silkscreen
Founder and CEO, AIR-igate, Inc.**

AIR-IGATE STOCK

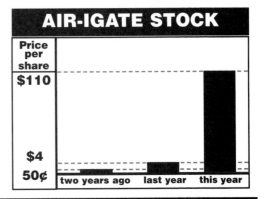

Price per share		
$110		
$4		
50¢		
two years ago	last year	this year

STOCK ANALYSIS: Profits depend entirely on worldwide approval of rain alternative, lack of competition, greed, graft, and cooperation from the U.S. Congress.

The AIR-igate Model for Success

1. We begin with only the purest mountain water from China and combine it with water from unscheduled rain events.

Bags capture old-fashioned rain.

2. Biodegradable balloons are filled with water and loaded into AIR-igate planes.

Planes are fueled with renewable gas alternative at our private airport.

3. Our water balloons are dropped at night.

Water drops!

4. The cycle of life continues!

5. Renewable resources are returned to the environment via our nonprofit subsidiary.

"AIR-igation is like a faucet we can turn on and off."
—CEO Snedley P. Silkscreen

Learn more about this and other exciting developments at the
**AIR-IGATE annual shareholders' meeting
this year in Sinkiang, China!**

WE'LL BE THINKING IN SINKIANG!

TODAY'S ASSIGNMENT:

Let's debate pros/cons of investing our class-trip fund in the stock market.

PROS	CONS
Possibility of making a lot of money fast	Risk of losing it all—fast
Seems sorta fun & exciting!	If we lose, ~~sorta~~ COMPLETELY awful
AIR-igate looks like a safe investment	What about the fine print?
Proven track record	

What else is there to invest in?

Wish we could invest in Florence.

Bring in beans for BLAST! drive.

Beans Lift Am___ Spirit Tr___usly!

<u>**FACSIMILE**</u>

From the law offices of
Sharks, Sharks, and Sharks
1-800-GO-4BLOOD

Barry Cuda
Attorney-at-Law

January 31

Walter Russ
Principal
Geyser Creek Middle School
Geyser Creek, Missouri

Wally:

Based on our discussion earlier today, I suggest you call a press conference. I'll handle the media.

Barry Cuda

P.S. Here's my idea for your new sink:

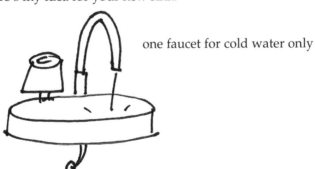

one faucet for cold water only

Maybe that way I can keep my clients out of hot water.

✴THE GEYSER CREEK GAZETTE✴

Our motto: "We have a nose for news!"

Wednesday, February 2   **50 cents**

EXCLUSIVE: Scandal at Middle School!
Principal sunk sink money in sinkhole

In an exclusive investigation, the *Geyser Creek Gazette* has learned that Geyser Creek Middle School Principal Walter Russ sunk the school's entire $500 sink fund in Rainy-Day Rainwear, a company that has lost 99.89% percent of its value since September.

With only 55 cents left in the sink fund, plans for the new sink in the school cafeteria are down the drain.

Ima Crabbie said yesterday she is not surprised by the news of her only son's investment blunder.

"That lunkhead nearly lost all my money, too!" carped Crabbie, who now manages her own finances.

Others were stunned by the news.

"It's one thing to gamble with his own money, but to invest the school's money so recklessly is another story," said barber Fisher Cutbait. "Where were the principal's principles?"

Attorney Barry Cuda said his client will write a "rain check" for the money.

"Wally has promised to pay back the school in full," Cuda said. "It may take time, but he'll do it."

Wall Street analysts often call losing investments like Rainy-Day Rainwear *financial sinkholes* because they trap unwary investors who have difficulty escaping unharmed from the rapid drop.

Meanwhile, the sink situation continues to worsen at Geyser Creek Middle School. Reports indicate the sink is now 80 percent clogged.

How Wally's Investment of Sink Funds Tanked

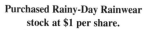

Purchased Rainy-Day Rainwear stock at $1 per share.

500 shares were worth $500.

Now 500 shares are worth only 55¢.

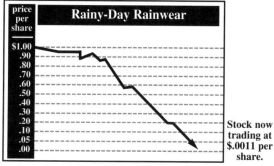

Stock now trading at $.0011 per share.

Attorney Barry Cuda read the following statement at yesterday's press conference:

"My client Walter 'Wally' Russ takes full responsibility for poorly investing the money set aside for the new sink. In September he bought 500 shares of Rainy-Day Rainwear stock for $1 per share. He intended to sell the stock when it went up, hoping to make a small profit for the school, which everyone knows is suffering under the current budget cutbacks. Sadly, the stock sunk even lower. If it's any consolation, you should know that Wally lost a considerable amount of his own money in the stock. His retirement money was invested entirely in 1,000 shares of Rainy-Day Rainwear, which are now worth exactly $1.10 total."

Missouri Farmers Demand AIR-igation

Environmentalists complain about smell of fake rain

Missouri farmers want AIR-igation and they want it now, according to Sen. Sue Ergass (I-MO), who introduced legislation in Congress to fast-track approval of the new rain alternative.

"Why must my constituents endure rainy days when all across Europe and Asia AIR-igation has replaced rain?" Ergass asked during a congressional hearing yesterday.

AIR-igation is still under review by the Stimulating Indigenous Natural Know-how (SINK) Committee in the U.S. Senate. Yesterday the committee heard testimony from several environmental groups that are lobbying aggressively to block approval of AIR-igation.

"Some of us happen to like rainy days," said Al Natchral, leader of We Enjoy Thunderstorms (WET), a grassroots environmental organization dedicated to saving the rain. "Besides, I've traveled to countries that are using AIR-igation, and I can tell you that the smell packs quite a punch. It knocked me out cold."

AIR-igation was invented by Missouri's own Snedley P. Silkscreen, a former dairy farmer.

Mail Salvaged from Sunken Ship; Fish Suffer Hardship

Geyser Creek Postmaster Carrie N. Urmayle says a letter addressed to Geyser Creek was salvaged from sunken ship.

The U.S. Postal Service has recovered most of the mail that was aboard the SS *Sinkiang* when it sank in September.

"All of our mail containers are waterproof and fireproof," U.S. Postmaster General Phil Atelic said yesterday. "Some of the mail was damaged, but we're doing our best to deliver it to the addresses we can read."

A ship sailing from China sank in September when an explosion ignited the vessel, killing all aboard and damaging much of the cargo. Authorities have not determined the cause of the explosion. Scientists say the fumes and sullied waters are causing fish in surrounding waters to suffer a combination of stress, fatigue, and depression.

"The fumes and stagnant waters are choking the fish and breaking their spirits," said aquaculturist Marina Byologee.

Wall Street Wrap-up

Stocks to Watch	Yesterday's	Opening price:	Closing price:	Change:
	AIR-igate, Inc.	$122.00	$173.24	+42%
	Dyeing to Please	$4.26	$4.64	+9%
	Glum Gum	$1.19	$ .95	-20%
	Rainy-Day Rainwear	$ .0019	$ .0011	-42%
	Tough Beans	$6.14	$8.29	+35%

Because I Said So!
By U.S. Senator Sue Ergass

Dear Senator Sue:
Is milk necessary for growing children?
Please tell me.
Wy, Winona, MO

Dear Wy in Winona:

Of course milk isn't necessary! Beans are the best nourishment for children. They're high in protein and low in fat. Beans are nature's perfect food!

Speaking of beans, I'm happy to announce that I'll be delivering the lovely legumes to the Chinese people next week when I travel to Asia.

It's all part of my "I'm Here, I'm MOM—How Can I Help?" tour.

So, keep collecting beans. And why not make a big bowl of 21-bean soup for dinner tonight?

Why, Wy? Because I said so!

The Honorable Sue Ergass,
"Senator MOM"
More Opportunities for Missourians

Investor's Corner

By Macon Bigbucks, Investment Counselor

How do you know when to hold and when to fold when you own a stock that's rapidly losing value? It's a personal decision. Some investors are content to weather financial storms in the hopes of long-term payoffs. More cautious investors seek shelter at the earliest sign of a downturn by selling, even if it means taking a loss.

My advice? You don't lose anything until you sell. And if you wait too long and the stock sinks to zero? Well, then you've got nothing to lose!

U.S. POSTAL SERVICE
Geyser Creek, Missouri

Our motto: "Neither rain, nor snow, nor sleet, nor hail, nor dark of night will stay these faithful couriers from the swift completion of their appointed rounds."

February 2

Mr. Sam N.'s Sixth-Grade Class
Geyser Creek Middle School
Geyser Creek, Missouri

SUBJECT: Item Found Loose in the Mail

Dear Sixth-Grade Class:

The enclosed was found loose in the mail in its present condition. We are forwarding it to the only address available.

If you have any questions, please contact me or the Claims Section of the U.S. Postal Service.

Sincerely,

Carrie N. Urmayle

Carrie N. Urmayle
Postmaster, Geyser Creek

P. S. Looks like a letter from Florence! Hurrah!

XINJIANG INN

September 20

Mr. Sam N.'s Sixth-Grade Class
Geyser Creek Middle School
Geyser Creek, Missouri

Hello from Xinjiang (also spelled Sinkiang)!

What a fascinating place! Are you familiar with the Taklamakan
Desert? It's in the center of the Tarim Basin. Imagine my surprise
when I learned that the Taklamakan Desert is known as the Sea of
Death from which nobody can escape. Well!

The days can be boiling hot and the nights freezing cold. Streams
flow into the desert basin but then evaporate. Not very helpful to
the farmers, who desperately need the water. Lots of talk here about
AIR-igation. I'm eager to see how it works! Then I've got to catch my
ride home. I'm sailing on the SS *Sinkiang*.

I do love a good adventure, don't you? Oh, did I mention the fre-
quent sand storms and poisonous snakes? Who knew researching
sinks would be so exciting? But goodness knows, you don't have to
travel around the globe to find adventure. Do you know where the
very best adventures in the world are? Right under your nose. It's
true! Some of my favorite adventures have taken place in my own
backyard or while sharing a meal with friends. Speaking of which,
I'm looking forward to seeing all of YOU again very soon and discussing your new sink.

Yours in adventures—and good *feng shui,*

XO *Florence Waters*

P.S. Please tell your principal that I'm NOT mad at him for calling me
filthy and unnecessary Waters. In fact, I'd like to bring him a little
present. Have you heard of the Sinkiang Blinking Spotted Suckerfish? I've read this fish is very close to extinction. I'll try to export
a pair. We could combine the sink with a wildlife refuge for the fish!
I'll sketch a picture of what I mean.

P.P.S. to Sam N.: No suckerfish for you. But don't worry. There
are other fish in the sea. The one I have in mind for you is a real
treasure.

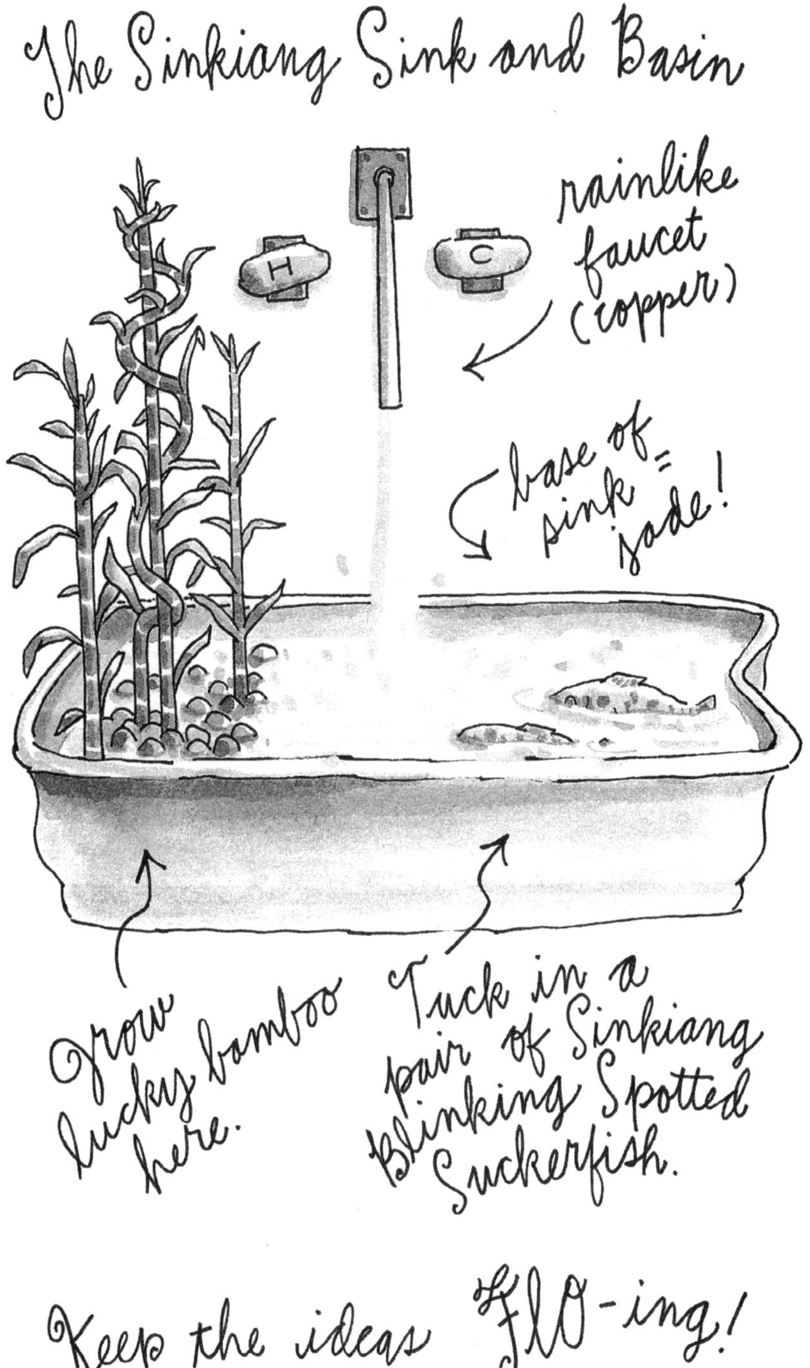

The Sinkiang Sink and Basin

rainlike
faucet
(copper)

base of
sink =
jade!

H

C

Grow
lucky bamboo
here.

Tuck in a
pair of Sinkiang
Blinking Spotted
Suckerfish.

Keep the ideas FLO-ing!

GEYSER CREEK MIDDLE SCHOOL
SIXTH-GRADE CLASS
Geyser Creek, Missouri
Our NEW class motto: "It's going to be a long hard drag, but we'll make it." —Janis Joplin

February 4

Ms. A. V. Aytor
c/o Flowing Waters Fountains, Etc.
Watertown, California

Dear Ms. Aytor,

Look at this letter we just received from Florence. We've GOT to go to Sinkiang to look for her!

That's why we're writing to you. Is there any chance you could fly us to China? We know it's a lot to ask, but we've raised $123.97 for our class-trip fund and would gladly pay you that.

Will you think about it and let us know?

Thanks a million!

Your friends,

Lily   Tad

Minnie O.

Paddy   Gil

Shelly

A. V. Aytor

February 7

Mr. Sam N.'s Sixth-Grade Class
Geyser Creek Middle School
Geyser Creek, Missouri

Dear friends,

Amazing! Of course we should go to China to look for Florence! But there's a problem: money.

International flights require a beastly amount of jet fuel. That will be our biggest expense. We'll also want to take rescue equipment, cameras, and radios. You'll all need passports. We'll have landing fees and hotel bills in China . . . plus insurance. And we should have some extra cash for unexpected expenses.

I'm afraid I wouldn't feel comfortable taking this trip with less than $100,000. And unfortunately, I haven't had a paycheck since Florence left. What savings I did have I've spent paying all the bills that keep pouring in.

I suppose I could try to sell some of Florence's things. Anything belonging to Florence would bring a tidy sum, especially if people know she might be . . .

Ugh. I can't bear to think about that. What should we do?

Sincerely,

A. V.

Ariel Veronica Aytor

P.S. How strange that Florence mentioned the Sinkiang Blinking Spotted Suckerfish. I was just reading about it. Florence had a stack of books and magazines on her nightstand. On top was the *Congressional Record*. It was opened to this page.

Actual testimony from CONGRESSIONAL HEARING

SENATOR ERGASS. Ladies and Gentlemen on both sides of the aisle, I am proud—PROUD!—to designate TODAY, SEPTEMBER 13, Take a Sinkiang Blinking Spotted Suckerfish to Lunch Day! I see some of you look surprised. I see—What's this?—a little chuckling from my distinguished colleague from South Dakota? Well, chuckle not, friends. Because once you know more about the Sinkiang Blinking Spotted Suckerfish, you will not laugh. No, you will cry. Why? Because this sweet fish is months, perhaps just weeks, away from extinction. What? This is the first you've heard of it? I'm not surprised. Cats. Dogs. Gerbils. Goldfish. They all have powerful lobbies. Who will speak for the Sinkiang Blinking Spotted Suckerfish? Look, friends, we've all had pets. But not one is more loyal than the Sinkiang Blinking Spotted Suckerfish. Unfortunately, the poor people of Sinkiang, China, aren't protecting this creature like they should. They're eating it to extinction!

PARLIAMENTARIAN. Thirty seconds, Senator Ergass.

SENATOR ERGASS. Thirty seconds? I'll be [DELETED]. Okay, people. I'll make it real simple. This is your MOM talking. There's this fish over in China, see, that's gonna be extinct if we don't step in and take some action. I won't bore you with the details, but I know people who can help. Folks, it's not that complicated. Just raise your stubby little hand if you're in favor of adding the Sinkiang Blinking Spotted Suckerfish to the Federal list of endangered species. . . . 94, 95, 96, 97. Texas? Thank you. 98, 99. I'll make it 100. Okay, and keep those hands in the air while I make a motion—Be a good boy and second it; thank you!—for a special appropriation to fund the Eeny-Meany-Miney-MO Beans, MO Pork, MO Money for Missouri bill, which will send another 200 million pounds of Missouri beans to the Chinese so they can eat beans instead of this poor little endangered fish. Okey-dokey! And keep those hands up for a commemorative postage stamp, too, with my picture on it and a little old international airport in Sinkiang for my pal Snedley P. Silkscreen. Good boys!

PARLIAMENTARIAN. Time expired, Senator Ergass.

SENATOR ERGASS. I don't like that tone in your voice, young man.

Addition to ENDANGERED SPECIES LIST

As defined by the U.S. Congress,
amended on this 13th day of September
to include the
Sinkiang Blinking Spotted Suckerfish

WHEREAS, the Sinkiang Blinking Spotted Suckerfish is a defenseless creature with no one to protect it but us, and

WHEREAS, its only natural environment is in Sinkiang, China, and

WHEREAS, the people of China are threatening the very existence of this rare fish by eating it:

It is RESOLVED that the United States of America make every effort to protect this species from extinction lest the international ecosystem go down the drain.

And while we're at it, let's send some Missouri beans over to those folks in China.

Therefore and henceforth and without further Congressional whoop-de-do, we hereby establish and forevermore fund the

International Project to Protect
the Sinkiang Blinking Spotted Suckerfish

and all that entails, including but not limited to tax credits, free parking, dry cleaning, and gum for our friends and supporters.

GEYSER CREEK MIDDLE SCHOOL
SIXTH-GRADE CLASS
Geyser Creek, Missouri
Our NEW class motto: "Where there is great love there are always miracles." —Willa Cather

February 8

Ms. A. V. Aytor
c/o Flowing Waters Fountains, Etc.
Watertown, California

Dear A.V.,

THANKS for the information! And don't worry about the $100,000. We'll raise it somehow.

Your friends,

Lily

Paddy

Shelly

Gil

Minnie O.

Tad

Sixth-Grade Class to Hold Silent Auction

Sixth-grade students at Geyser Creek Middle School yesterday announced plans for a silent auction to be held on Monday, February 14, at the Geyser Creek Cafe to raise money for their class trip.

Only one item will be auctioned off: a letter Florence Waters wrote in September to Geyser Creek Middle School Principal Walter Russ.

"We hope to raise $100,000," said Tad Poll, who acknowledged the class had mixed feelings about parting with the letter. "It's hard to let go of something as priceless as this. But it's one of our most valuable assets, and we decided we're willing to auction it for a good cause."

Poll said Russ gave the letter to the sixth-grade class and has no interest in it. The students have not announced where they plan to travel on their class trip. Speaking on the condition of anonymity, one student said: "We don't want to spill the beans, so we'll just say we're going to follow the waters." Another student reported: "We're going to follow our hearts."

Financial experts question the students' ability to raise $100,000 with the letter.

"There's a fine line between priceless and worthless," said investment counselor Macon Bigbucks.

The letter will be on display through February 14 at the Geyser Creek Cafe.

Students announce plans for silent auction.

Sen. Sue Ergass Takes Her White-Glove Test to China

"Hot rollers, honey. Trust me."

"You put some pumps with that, and you've got yourself an outfit."

Because I Said So!

By U.S. Senator Sue Ergass

Dear Senator Sue:
Where are you and what are you doing?
C. More, Seymour, MO
P.S. Gosh, you're pretty!

Dear Seymour C. More:

I'm over here in China, where I've fast-tracked funding to protect the endangered Sinkiang Blinking Spotted Suckerfish, the friendly fish with the spots that blinks as a way of showing its appreciation for all I've done to protect it.

Mother Nature did her best. Now it's MOM to the rescue.

I'll be home soon.

Have a bean burrito for your pretty MOM. Why? Because I said so!

The Honorable Sue Ergass,
"Senator MOM"
More Opportunities for Missourians

Wall Street Wrap-up

Stocks to Watch

Yesterday's	Opening price:	Closing price:	Change:
AIR-igate, Inc.	$189.00	$255.15	+35%
Dyeing to Please	$5.35	$6.52	+22%
Glum Gum	$1.23	$1.14	-7%
Rainy-Day Rainwear	$ .0010	$ .0009	-10%
Tough Beans	$10.47	$13.40	+28%

Sink Aroma Leaves Students in Near Coma

Sink now 98% clogged, 100% stinky

The smell from the clogged sink in the Geyser Creek Middle School cafeteria has caused several students to become tired, run-down, depressed, and unable to focus on their studies.

"The fumes from the sink could be used in stink bombs," said Gil, a sixth-grade student who passed out cold yesterday when he walked into the cafeteria for lunch.

Unfortunately, there are no funds to repair or replace the sink, which is now 98 percent clogged.

"We're using air freshener and fans to circulate the stale air," said Principal Walter Russ. "Students may wish to wear gas masks to protect themselves from the sink stink."

Why Is Ima Crabbie Less Crabby? Kids and Carp

No, it's not your imagination.

Ima Crabbie *is* less crabby.

Crabbie watchers attribute her better mood to local sixth graders, who have been helping the octogenarian spiff up the Geyser Creek Senior Home.

"I saw Ima and those kids down at the pond yesterday, laughing and fishing," a resident of the home said yesterday. "She was actually smiling."

Crabbie hired the students to help her stock the pond behind the retirement home with grass carp to aerate the pond and eliminate tall weeds and algae. While working with the students, Crabbie has been teaching her young friends about investing in the stock market.

"It gets her mind off her son," said another resident. "You don't want to ask Ima how much of her money Wally lost. That's the one subject that still makes Ima crabby."

In exchange for helping her stock the pond, Crabbie teaches students about stocks and bonds.

GEYSER CREEK MIDDLE SCHOOL

Geyser Creek, Missouri

Sam N.
Sixth-Grade Teacher

My motto: "You will do foolish things, but do them with enthusiasm." —Colette

February 10

Mr. Russ:

Has a sixth-grade class ever traveled out of the state on a class trip? What about out of the country? The continent?

Mr. N.

BEAN-MAIL
Brief Educational and/or Administrative Note

My motto: "We are [still] not amused." —Queen Victoria

To: Mr. Sam N.
Fr: Principal Walter Russ
Re: No
Date: February 11
Time: 8:22 A.M.

No, no, and no.

I'm in NO mood for jokes, Mr. N., especially
from someone who refuses to use his bean to
employ his LIMA to send BEAN-mail. (Mr. N.,
if you can *receive* BEAN-mail, you can *send*
BEAN-mail. Simply click on the SEND BEAN icon.)

Unless I hear otherwise, I'll assume the silent
auction is just another prank.

On a more serious note, your students might
consider a silent *class* for a change. The noise
from your classroom combined with the smell from
the cafeteria is giving me a ~~sink~~ SICK headache
and chest pains.

♥

It's Valentine's Day!
So do your HEART a favor. . . .

What better way to celebrate this day of love and friendship than by bidding on a letter from Geyser Creek's *best friend*, Florence Waters? Please indicate your bid in the space provided. You may bid as often as you like. The highest bidder at 5:00 P.M. will be the new owner of this priceless letter. Thank you for your support!

—The Sixth-Grade Class
Geyser Creek Middle School

SILENT AUCTION

Bid	Time	Amount	Bidder
1.	6:30 A.M.	$10	Angel Fisch
2.	7:05 A.M.	$15	Pearl O. Ster
3.	7:45 A.M.	$100	Goldie Fisch
4.	8:30 A.M.	$125	Pearl O. Ster
5.	9:12 A.M.	$135	Barry Cuda
6.	10:30 A.M.	$150	CeCe Salt
7.	11:10 A.M.	$165	Sting Raye
8.	11:40 A.M.	$200	Sam N.
9.	11:41 A.M.	$225	Fisher Cutbait

Geyser Creek Senior Home

Just a Note to Say... This Is Your Lucky Day!

SOMEONE CALLED YOU!

MESSAGE FOR: Mrs. Crabbie

DATE: 2/14

TIME: 11:45 A.M.

Your son, Wally, is trying to get in touch with you. Please call him back. ~~NO~~

Geyser Creek Senior Home

Just a Note to Say... This Is Your Lucky Day!

SOMEONE CALLED YOU!

MESSAGE FOR: Mrs. Crabbie

DATE: 2/14

TIME: 1:20 P.M.

Wally called again. Will you please call him?

~~DON'T MAKE ME REPEAT MYSELF.~~

Geyser Creek Senior Home

Just a Note to Say... This Is Your Lucky Day!

SOMEONE CALLED YOU!

MESSAGE FOR: Mrs. Crabbie

DATE: 2/14

TIME: 3:15 P.M.

Sorry, but Wally called again. Says he needs to speak with you about something very important. Can he stop by your apartment? NO.

He's coming anyway.

SILENT AUCTION

Bid	Time	Amount	Bidder
79.	3:35 P.M.	$1,250	Annette Trap
80.	3:58 P.M.	$1,500	Sam N.
81.	4:10 P.M.	$1,750	Anne Chovey
82.	4:30 P.M.	$2,000	Mayor I. B. Newt
83.	4:45 P.M.	$2,005	Sam N.
84.	4:50 P.M.	$2,010	Goldie Fisch
85.	4:58 P.M.	$2,015	Pearl O. Ster

FACSIMILE

FIRST BANK OF GEYSER CREEK
Geyser Creek, Missouri

Juan A. Lone
President

DATE: February 14
TO: Sixth-Grade Class, Geyser Creek Middle School
            c/o Geyser Creek Cafe
FR: Juan A. Lone
RE: Bid

I have received instructions to place a $100,000 bid for the item currently on the auction block.

If this is the highest bid, please contact me so that I can issue you a check in exchange for the letter.

There is one nonnegotiable condition on this offer: the buyer must remain anonymous.

Thank you.

Juan A. Lone

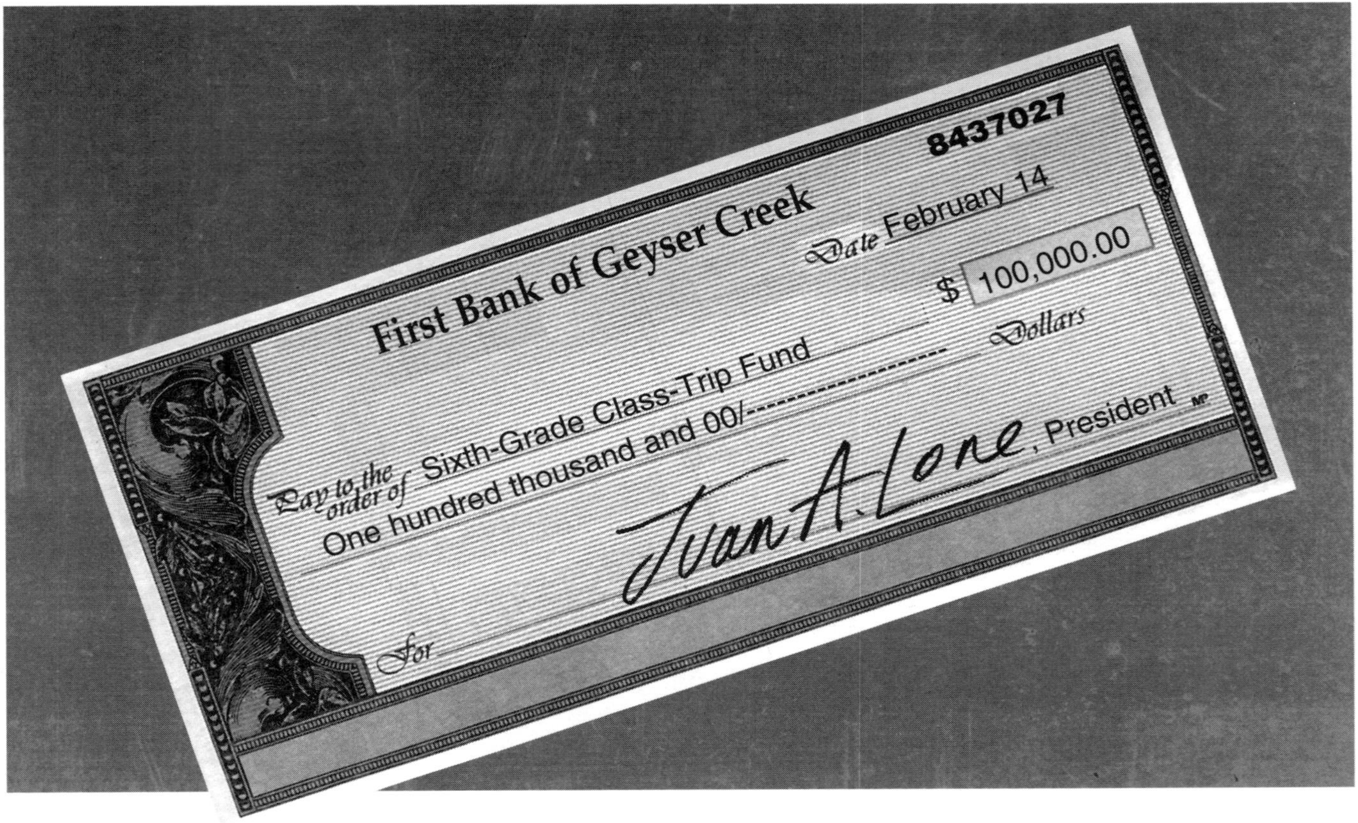

First Bank of Geyser Creek

8437027

Date February 14

Pay to the
order of   Sixth-Grade Class-Trip Fund

$ 100,000.00

One hundred thousand and 00/-   Dollars

For   Stan Alone, President

Geyser Creek Middle School
Geyser Creek, Missouri

A.V.,

How soon can you get
to Geyser Creek?

Meet us here.

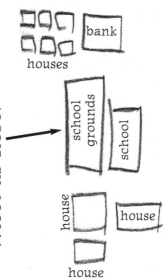

houses

bank

school grounds

school

house

house

house

Ms. Ariel Veronica Aytor
c/o Flowing Waters Fountains, Etc.
Watertown, California

HOT-LUNCH MENU: bean soup

TODAY'S ASSIGNMENTS:

- Schedule appt. with   **Gil 2:00** P.M.**!**
  passport photographer.   *Tad*
- Make hotel reservations.
- Collect all of our Florence *Lily*
  research in one binder.   *Paddy*
- Ditto all of our Sinkiang info.
- Find out if we need shots.   Gil   NO!—thank goodness
- Figure out our route.   *Minnie O.*
- Make sure ALL permission
  slips are in by tomorrow.   *Shelly*

WORD/SYMBOL OF THE DAY: 危機

In Chinese the symbol representing <u>crisis</u> is a combination of the figures for <u>danger</u> and <u>opportunity</u>.

B__ng in b__ns for B____ drive.

B____ Lift A__ Spirit T__ sly!

maps
binoculars
cameras
tape recorders
notebooks/pens/paper
English-Chinese
    dictionary
Florence's sketches

Don't forget

GEYSER CREEK MIDDLE SCHOOL
Geyser Creek, Missouri

From the Desk of Goldie Fisch

*My motto: "A man has to be Joe McCarthy to be called ruthless.
All a woman has to do is put you on hold." —Marlo Thomas*

February 15

Tad and Lily:

Mrs. Crabbie called again to ask if you could help her with
some chores this afternoon. Do you mind? I know she'd
appreciate it.

Thanks.

Goldie

Geyser Creek Senior Home

Old Pond Road   *Geyser Creek, Missouri*

My motto: "I'll give you something to cry about." —Imogene Crabbie

February 15

Sixth-Grade Stinkers
Geyser Creek Middle School
Geyser Creek, Missouri

Tad and Lily:

You dumdums! You forgot to give me a bill today. Here's $20. That should cover it.

I still don't understand how you intend to pay for your trip to China. Do you think money grows on trees?

Well, if you do go to China, promise me two things:

1. You'll go to the AIR-igate Annual Shareholders' Meeting. Here's my proxy card; you'll need it to get in.

2. The minute you get back from your trip, you'll come over here and tell me all about it.

That's all, except lookit: Don't you dare get hurt over there. You're the cheapest labor in town.

Imogene Crabbie
Imogene Crabbie

P.S. Hey, I've got a new motto: "Maturity only enhances mystery, never decreases it." —Emily Dickinson

AIR-IGATE, INC.
•••••••••••••••••••••••••
Delivering Water by AIR...   Because We CARE!

Imogene Crabbie
Geyser Creek Senior Home
Old Pond Road
Geyser Creek, Missouri

Dear Valued Shareholder:

You are invited to attend the annual meeting of AIR-igate, Inc., shareholders to be held at 10:00 A.M. on February 22 at the Sinkiang Inn in Sinkiang, China.

Attendance at the annual meeting is limited to AIR-igate, Inc., shareholders, members of their immediate families, or their designated representative(s).

Yours in cash flows,

Snedley P. Silkscreen

Snedley P. Silkscreen
Founder and CEO, AIR-igate, Inc.

P.S. Enclosed is an AIR-igate, Inc., gas mask to protect you from airborne germs.

PROXY

I, IMOGENE CRABBIE, hereby appoint the following person(s) to serve as my representative(s) at the AIR-igate, Inc., annual meeting on February 22.

The stinking brats in the sixth-grade class at Geyser Creek Middle School.

AIR-igate founder and CEO Snedley P. Silkscreen will speak to shareholders, followed by our keynote speaker, U.S. Senator Sue Ergass (I-MO).

GEYSER CREEK MIDDLE SCHOOL
Geyser Creek, Missouri

Sam N.
Sixth-Grade Teacher

My new motto: "Life shrinks or expands in proportion to one's courage." —Anaïs Nin

February 16

Principal Russ:

I'm pleased to report that due to your generous contribution of Florence's letter and an equally generous payment from an anonymous donor to purchase the letter, my students have raised enough money to travel to Sinkiang, China, for their class trip.

Permission slips from all the parents are attached. Isn't it wonderful to have their confidence and support for this exciting trip? Your leadership has really helped.

The students will be happy to give you a full report of their trip when we return to Geyser Creek later this month or possibly early next, but certainly before the end of the school year.

Let us know if there's anything special you'd like us to bring you from China. After all, without your generous donation of the letter from Florence, none of this would be possible.

Sincerely,

Sam N.

BEAN-MAIL
Brief Educational and/or Administrative Note

My new motto: "Power is the ability not to have to please." —Elizabeth Janeway

```
To:    Mr. Sam N.
Fr:    Walter Russ
Re:    Class trip
Date:  February 17
Time:  9:15 A.M.
```

This little game has gone on long enough, Mr. N.

Surely you are aware of Missouri Middle-School Mindless Middle Management Finance Regulation 18PPW-LTVZ, which prohibits schools from accepting large financial contributions from anonymous sources.

To protect myself and this school from a possible lawsuit, I must tell you in NO uncertain terms that you do NOT have my permission or that of the school to take your students to China (*China?!*) on this madcap adventure.

If you do, Mr. N., you can be assured that you will NOT have a job when you return. Missouri Middle-School Mindless Middle Management Administrative Regulation 1022-LTVZ prohibits employment of teachers who violate Missouri Middle-School Mindless Middle Management Finance Regulation 18PPW-LTVZ.

Another thing: You're the only teacher who refuses to send BEAN-mail despite my repeated requests. An Insubordination Report will be added to your permanent file.

And where are your beans, Mr. N.? I noticed yours was the only class that missed the deadline for the bean drive.

GEYSER CREEK MIDDLE SCHOOL
Geyser Creek, Missouri

Sam N.
Sixth-Grade Teacher

My new motto: "And the trouble is, if you don't risk anything, you risk even more."
—Erica Jong

February 18

Principal Russ:

You made your point. And maybe you're right. But I've got a job to do. And that job is believing in these kids. ~~They~~ *We* believe in Florence. And we're going to find her. If that means my job is down the drain . . . Well, so be it.

I'm not much for dramatic exits, but I can tell you this: A person's job isn't worth a hill of beans in this crazy world. Someday you'll understand that, Mr. Russ. Maybe not today. Maybe not tomorrow. But I hope someday you find something or someone you believe in enough to take a risk on—besides rainwear investments.

I haven't told my students this, but I'll tell you: I'm afraid Florence is dead at sea. In her last letter to us, she wrote that she planned to return home on the SS *Sinkiang*, the ship that sank in September. No survivors were found.

Maybe it's too late to save Florence, but we've got to try. Sometimes you just have to go with the Flo. Or at least I do.

Along with the Insubordination Report, please add the attached resignation to my permanent file.

The students will deliver their beans to China themselves.

Good-bye, Mr. Russ. Also attached is a final idea regarding the sink.

Sam N.

OFFICIAL RESIGNATION FORM

I, _____Sam N._____ , hereby submit my
resignation from the position of _sixth-grade teacher_
for the reason(s) described below:

_____

_____

Creative differences with
school administration

No need to read,
Mr. Russ.

Goldie

_____

_____

My resignation shall be effective

at the end of current school year.

Signature_____Sam N._____
Date_____Feb. 18_____

GEYSER CREEK MIDDLE SCHOOL

LETTERS

The Florence Waters Memorial Sink
The Art of Flo

☆THE GEYSER CREEK GAZETTE☆

Our motto: "We have a nose for news!"

Saturday, February 19   50 cents

Explosion Rocks Cafeteria as Sixth Graders Depart for China

An explosion rocked the Geyser Creek Middle School last night, ripping the cafeteria sink off a wall.

"Guess that solved the clog problem," said school secretary Goldie Fisch.

No injuries were reported. Authorities have not determined the cause of the explosion, which occurred at about 8:00 P.M.

Equally dramatic was the sudden departure of the entire Geyser Creek Middle School sixth-grade class for Sinkiang, China. Defying Principal Walter Russ, six students and one teacher boarded a private plane that landed shortly after 9:00 P.M. behind the school.

Many view the unauthorized class trip as one more indication of Principal Walter Russ's sinking credibility in Geyser Creek.

"I don't blame the kids one iota for disobeying their principal," said Ima Crabbie, Russ's mother. "How can you respect a man who sunk all of his money in raincoats?"

It is not clear when the students plan to return.

Students and teacher depart for China while firefighters respond to an explosion in school cafeteria.

Identity of Bidder Still Unknown

The identity of the anonymous bidder at last Monday's silent auction fund-raiser for the Geyser Creek Middle School sixth-grade class remains a mystery.

According to sources in the Geyser Creek financial community, only a few local residents have enough liquid assets to cover a $100,000 bid.

"When we talk about liquid assets, we're talking about cash on hand," investment counselor Macon Bigbucks explained yesterday.

An unnamed source said the likely donor was the unlikable Ima Crabbie.

"Everybody knows Ima's got money to burn," said one observer. "Plus, she's gotten to know those kids over the past few months. I can see her bidding on the letter just to tick off her son, Wally Russ."

Mrs. Crabbie refused to say whether she paid $100,000 for the letter.

"It's none of your dadjing business," she told reporters.

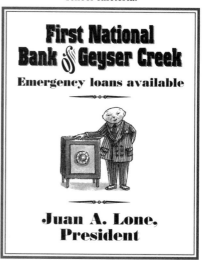

Protestors Say AIR-igation Leads to Angina; "Senator MOM" Tours China

(WASHINGTON) Environmentalists opposed to AIR-igation marched on Washington yesterday as the Stimulating Indigenous Natural Know-how (SINK) Committee of the U.S. Senate heard more testimony regarding the possible side effects of the rain alternative.

"The rain in Spain smells mainly like propane, while the stinking in Sinkiang is growing, not shrinking," chanted members of We Enjoy Thunderstorms (WET), a grassroots environmental organization dedicated to saving the rain.

WET spokesperson Al Natchral told the SINK Committee that AIR-igation produces toxic fumes, which can contribute to fainting spells, strokes, and angina.

SINK Committee member Sen. Sue Ergass was absent from the hearings. The Missouri senator is in China, delivering beans from her BLAST! drive and studying the effects of AIR-igation firsthand.

AIR-igation has not been approved for use in the U.S.

Because I Said So!

By U.S. Senator Sue Ergass

> **Dear Senator Sue:**
> You're my hero! What are you doing in China?
> **Hannah Belle, Hannibal, MO**

Dear Hannibal Hannah Belle:

I'm on a fact-finding mission to see how people over here like AIR-igation. Guess what? They love it! I'm doing all I can to bring AIR-igation to Missouri, including speaking at the AIR-igate, Inc., annual shareholders' meeting.

And here's more good news: Thanks to my efforts to provide an alternate source of protein for the Chinese people, the Sinkiang Blinking Spotted Suckerfish is making a comeback. Folks here in Sinkiang are finding the sweet little fish in rivers and ponds. Isn't that terrific? I'm pushing a supplemental "cool beans" appropriation through Congress so I can keep up the good work.

You can thank me later!

Why? Because I said so!

The Honorable Sue Ergass,
"Senator MOM"
More Opportunities for Missourians

Have you tried our hummus gummus?

Geyser Creek Cafe
No longer serving ice cream.
"It's just too expensive, folks."

Angel Fisch, Owner

"Here I am with my young Chinese fans!"

FLIGHT LOG

A. V. Aytor, Pilot
Departure date: Feb. 18
Departure time: 21:21:00
Destination: Sinkiang

VOICE-BOX RECORDING: This is A. V. Aytor, departing from Geyser Creek Middle School at 9:21 P.M. on a beautiful cloudless Friday evening. I'm carrying seven passengers who are fully briefed on safety issues. Our mission is to find Flo Waters in Sinkiang, China. How's Mr. N. doing back there?

MINNIE O.: His eyes are closed, but he says he's okay.

A. V. AYTOR: Tell him to relax. We're going with the Flo!

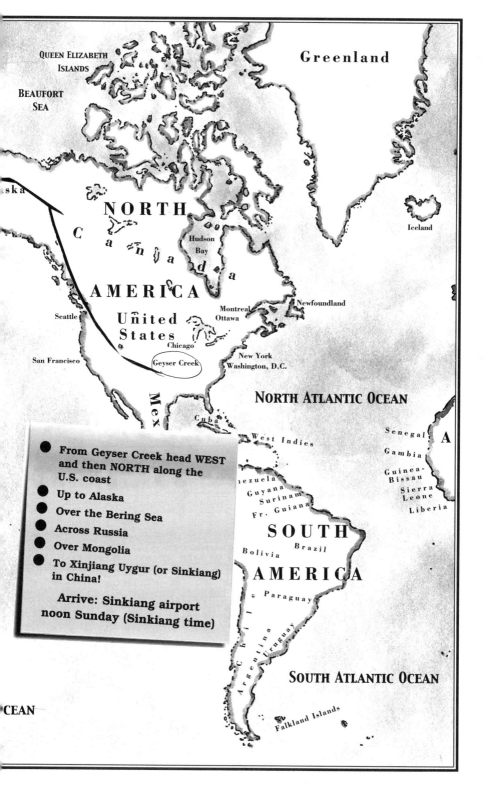

Welcome to the
XINJIANG INN
Today is Sunday, February 20.

WEATHER FORECAST: No rain today—and that's a guarantee! We're scheduled for AIR-igation at midnight tomorrow. It will last 22 minutes.

Welcome VIP Guest U.S. Senator Sue Ergass!

Reservation for Mr. Sam N.'s Sixth-Grade Class: five rooms

Room #	Guest(s)
212	Minnie & Shelly
213	Gil & Tad
214	Ms. Aytor
215	Lily & Paddy
216	Mr. N. & beans

Complimentary gas masks for hotel guests

XINJIANG INN

February 21

TODAY'S ASSIGNMENTS:

To find Florence, we should retrace her steps. Let's make a list of everything we know she did while in Sinkiang.

- She stayed at the Xinjiang Inn. *(So are we!)*

  Interview hotel employees.

  Shelly and Gil

- She was studying sinks and basins.

  Paddy   *We will, too!*

  Minnie O.

- She was looking for the rare Sinkiang Blinking Spotted Suckerfish.

  Tad and Lily   *We'll look, too.*

Divide up into research teams. Take cameras, notebooks, pens, and tape recorders. Meet back here at 6:00 P.M. with reports.

Somebody please deliver our beans to Senator Sue Ergass. She's staying in this hotel. —Mr. N.

95

Sinks and Basins
By Paddy and Minnie O.

The Tarim Basin is surrounded by the Tien Shan mountains to the north, the Pamir mountains to the west, and the Kunlun mountains to the south. The basin occupies more than half of Sinkiang, extending 850 miles from west to east and about 350 miles from north to south. The basin consists of a central desert, alluvial fans at the foot of the mountains, and isolated oases.

We know we're supposed to be thinking about sinks, but it's hard not to think about stinks. Sinkiang smells just like the cafeteria!

I'm trying to think like a sink,
because that's where Waters go.
I'm trying not to think of the stink,
so I'm holding my nose. —Minnie O.

Interviews with Hotel Staff
Shelly and Gil

Talked to a waitress and housekeeper; both said Florence was a very generous tipper. Also interviewed a desk clerk, who told us Florence left the hotel on the morning of September 20 but never returned.

Sinkiang Blinking Spotted Suckerfish
Tad and Lily

We looked in 17 different streams and rivers and couldn't find a single one. Just common grass carp, like the ones we put in the pond at the senior home.

BEAN-MAIL
Brief Educational and/or Administrative Note

To: Sam N.
Fr: Goldie Fisch
Re: Okay?
Date: February 21
Time: 9:17 A.M.

Sam,

I know you hate BEAN-mail, but I'm going crazy with worry.

You don't have to reply, but would you please ask one of your students to send me a quick BEAN-mail message to let me know you're all okay and that you've found Florence?

Thanks.

Goldie

P.S. Would it be okay for me to tell you I'm proud of you for what you're doing?

BEAN-MAIL
Brief Educational and/or Administrative Note

```
To:    Goldie Fisch
Fr:    Sam N.
Re:    Re: Okay?
Date:  February 22
Time:  12:30 A.M.
```

Dear Goldie,

I have to go to *China* to get a BEAN-mail message from you?

I'm kidding. I'm glad you wrote. But Goldie, I'm afraid you're going to be disappointed in me.

The students have done an amazing job following leads and gathering evidence. Still, no Florence.

I'm more discouraged than ever. Maybe it's the late hour or my fatigue. But I'm almost certain that Florence is dead.

Earlier tonight I sent the kids to deliver the canned beans to Senator Sue Ergass's hotel room. After that the only thing left for us to do is try to find a couple of Sinkiang Blinking Spotted Suckerfish. We decided to bring back a pair and raise them as a tribute to Florence.

I wish you were here, Goldie. We could use your smile. I've never had the opportunity--or the courage--to tell you this before, but in case I get hit by a rickshaw carrying a ton of beans tomorrow, I want you to know that your friendship means more to me than--

Drat. Someone's at my door.

Hi, Goldie! It's me, Paddy! Sorry to interrupt, but we need to talk to Mr. N.

Click on the attached audio and photo files to hear (and see!) what happened when we delivered our beans for the BLAST! drive to Senator Sue Ergass's hotel room.

Time recorded: 10:19 P.M.

SHELLY: Paddy, we're just dropping off our canned beans. You don't have to tape-record this.

PADDY: I know, but you never know what you might hear. Besides, I've got a gut feeling about this Senator Ergass.

GIL: Me, too. I brought my digital camera.

[KNOCK, KNOCK, KNOCK--SOUND OF DOOR OPENING]

SENATOR ERGASS: What do you want?

TAD: We have some beans for your BLAST! drive.

SENATOR ERGASS: My what?

GIL: Beans Lift America's Spirit Tremendously!

SENATOR ERGASS: Oh, right. Take the beans over to the AIR-igate complex. You can leave them at the back entrance near the barns.

LILY: Barns?

SENATOR ERGASS: Yes, BARNS! Now do what I say, and don't question authority. Children should be seen, not heard.

MINNIE O.: But why--?

SENATOR ERGASS: Because I said so! Now get those stinkin' beans out of my face and scram.

[SOUND OF DOOR SLAMMING]

FLIGHT LOG

A. V. Aytor, Pilot
Departure date: Feb. 21
Departure time: 23:58:00
Destination: Unknown

VOICE-BOX RECORDING: This is A. V. Aytor, reporting a departure time of just before midnight on Monday, taking off from the Sinkiang airport. Ten minutes ago I was sound asleep in my hotel room when six passengers woke me up, begging me to take them on a night flight over Sinkiang. My copilot is Paddy, who will take over from here.

PADDY: Hello, hello! Is this thing working? Okay. Well, I'm sitting with Ms. Aytor up front, where the view is much better. Sinkiang at night looks so different than it did earlier today. But the smell is even worse and—

[LOUD NOISE; INAUDIBLE CONVERSATION]

PADDY: Another plane is in the air! It's a—

[LOUD NOISE; INAUDIBLE CONVERSATION]

PADDY: Yes, it's definitely an AIR-igate, Inc., plane.

[LOUD NOISE; INAUDIBLE CONVERSATION]

LILY: Wow! That was close. Everybody okay? Paddy, I caught the tape recorder. Lily here, reporting that we just had a near miss with an AIR-igate, Inc., plane. We were so close, I could see the pilot, Snedley P. Silkscreen, and his passenger, Senator Sue Ergass. Is somebody getting photos of this? Thanks, Gil. We're following Silkscreen's plane as it drops huge water balloons over Sinkiang. The smell up here is beyond belief. And . . . wait. Now they're dropping something else. What the heck?

GIL: Ms. Aytor, can you get any closer, please, so we can get some pictures?

A.V.: I'm trying. Snedley's piloting his plane like a madman.

MINNIE O.: Wait a minute! Everybody look down right now! Do you see what I see?

SHELLY: Oh my gosh! It's—

[LOUD NOISE; INAUDIBLE CONVERSATION]

A.V.: Hang on, everybody! We're making an emergency landing.

XINJIANG INN

February 22

TODAY'S ASSIGNMENTS:

- **Care for our patient. Doctor says she needs rest, so let her sleep in.**

- **Have breakfast ready for her when she wakes up.** Lily

- **Print photos.** Gil

- **Contact Chinese authorities, U.S. embassy, media.** Paddy

- **Get in touch with animal-rescue officials.** Tad

- **Finish writing telegram by 8:00 A.M.** Minnie O. and Shelly

- **Rehearsal at 9:30 A.M.** Everyone!

WELCOME TO THE AIR-IGATE, INC., ANNUAL SHAREHOLDERS' MEETING!

SCHEDULE

Welcome:

Snedley P. Silkscreen, Founder and CEO
"The Future of AIR-igate: Diversification!"

Ceremonial burning of raincoats

Keynote address:

Our friend in Congress,
Senator Sue Ergass (I-MO)

AIR-IGATE, INC.
ANNUAL MEETING OF SHAREHOLDERS

KEYNOTE SPEAKER: U.S. SENATOR SUE ERGASS

SENATOR ERGASS: Thank you and welcome, investors! What a treat to have you gathered together in one room. You all pass my white-glove test with flying colors. And speaking of high fliers, wasn't Snedley P. Silkscreen's presentation positively inspiring? [Applause.] Yes, it was. Oh! What's this?

SHELLY: We have a singing telegram for you, Senator Ergass.

SENATOR ERGASS: For me? Oh! I bet it's from the boys in the Senate, telling me that AIR-igation has been approved for use in the United States. Let's hear it.

A ~~SINGING~~ SINKIANG TELEGRAM

**Written and Performed by the
Geyser Creek Middle School
Sixth-Grade Class**

Forgive us for interrupting
this annual meeting,
but we're here to deliver
an important greeting!

We begin with the story
of a fish with distinction:
"The Sinkiang Blinking Spotted
Suckerfish is *this* close to extinction!"

That was according
to Senator Sue,
who said she was certain
of what we must do.

"Send beans!" she said.
"It's as simple as that.
They're high in protein
and low in fat."

The beans came to China—
that much is true.
Not for the people
but for creatures that **moo.**

Cows—that's right!
Are you making the link?
Millions of cows
work for AIR-igate, Inc.

The cows are fed beans
Till their eyeballs **P O P !**
AIR-igate, Inc., is a
bovine sweatshop!

It's the natural gas
released by these cows
that fuels Silkscreen's planes,
which smell like yeeee-owwwwwwww!

It's this very same gas
from fermented legumes
that clogged our school sink
and caused the **KA-BOOM!**

So who has conducted
this flagrant corruption?
Who is behind all
these fragrant eruptions?

"Senator MOM," of course!
Who else could we mean?
She's the politician
who's full of beans!

She put beans on the menu
and in every lunch dish,
then she hand-painted spots
on thousands of fish!

Remove her white gloves,
and her hands testify
that she painted plain carp
with permanent dye!

Then she dropped them by air
from Silkscreen's airplanes
all over Asia—
it was inhumane!

So how did we catch
this windy gasbag?
How did we nab
this flatulent nag?

We used our beans
and followed the money!
Then we followed the beans
to a smell that was *funny.*

We learned the only thing better
than following your nose
is relying on the part of you
that always just knows:

It's not what people say;
it's the things that they *do.*
And the only business worth beans
is just trying to be true.

When you make that your job
and invest in a friend,
the payoff is priceless—
it's life's best dividend!

That's what we learned
from our friend Ms. Waters.
Go with the Flo!
It's our new alma mater!

For the heart always knows
where on earth it must go—
by following our hearts,
we found our friend Flo!

She knew we would find
where Waters goes;
she told us adventure is always
right under our nose.

So we dearly hope
that it's sinking in,
here at the lovely
Sinkiang Inn . . .

That we've come to the end
of our telegram.
So let's apprehend the stinkers
before they can **scram!**

EXTRADITION PAPERS

The following persons will be deported to the United States IMMEDIATELY to face federal charges under the Garbanzo Bean Accords of 1919, the U.N. Clean Air Act, and Article XVIII, Section 12, subsection (c) of the United States Code Annotated (USCA) Overseas Horrible Ghastly Asphyxiation by Gas (OHGAG) Act.

Hal E. Butt

Hal E. Butt
U.S. Attorney
St. Louis, Missouri
February 22

Silent (and violent!) partners in crime

Sue Ergass

No wonder she wore gloves—to hide her stained hands!

Sue Ergass was also charged with fabricating the letters that appeared in her advice column.

Snedley P. Silkscreen

No wonder he wore a gas mask—to protect himself from the stink he created!

Charges will also be filed against Silkscreen personally and his company, AIR-igate, Inc., for illegally transporting GASP gas, which led to last September's explosion on the SS *Sinkiang* that claimed the lives of all aboard and count-less fish. Silkscreen also faces charges of cruelty to animals at his cow sweatshop in Sinkiang.

SINKIANG NEWS

English edition

星期三　　　　　二月二十三日　　　　　二十五分錢

Now We Know What Was Stinking in Sinkiang!
Students find the stinky link: AIR-igate, Inc.

So *that's* what was stinking in Sinkiang: bean-fed cows, their natural by-product, and planes fueled by the bovine gas.

Or perhaps it's more accurate to say the real stinkers are Snedley P. Silkscreen, founder and CEO of AIR-igate, Inc., and U.S. Sen. Sue Ergass (I-MO).

Thanks to the Missouri senator's fishy story about the Sinkiang Blinking Spotted Suckerfish, Silkscreen was able to create the largest natural gas farm in the world.

The clandestine bovine sweatshop was uncovered by a group of sixth graders from Missouri who were in Sinkiang on a class trip. The students said they caught wind of the scam when they followed their noses—and some beans—to the source of the crime.

As the students' photographs show, the Missouri beans were delivered to the back gate of AIR-igate and fed to a herd of 7.2 million cows, resulting in the untold (and unseen) production of natural gas.

After authorities arrived on the scene, the students worked with world-famous fountain designer Florence Waters to free the cows from the AIR-igate complex.

The bean-fed cows produced the natural gas that fueled AIR-igate planes, which explains the odd smell associated with the rain alternative AIR-igation.

Legume *KA-BOOM!*

American students explained yesterday to international authorities how fermented beans created the gas that fueled Snedley P. Silkscreen's AIR-igate planes and caused explosions in their school cafeteria and aboard the SS *Sinkiang* last fall.

According to the sixth-grade students from Geyser Creek Middle School in Geyser Creek, Mo., Silkscreen's bovine sweatshop also accounted for the rise in milk prices.

Bean-fed cows produce foul-smelling fuel.

Silkscreen also sold the natural gas on the worldwide market through a nonprofit organization called Growers of Alternate Sources of Power (GASP), which contributed $100 million to Ergass's most recent political campaign.

"The smell here in Sinkiang reminded us of the smell in our school cafeteria back home," explained Paddy. "When we saw all those cows being force-fed beans at AIR-igate, we thought about all the beans served in our school cafeteria. Nobody ate them, so they were dumped down the sink, where they sat and fermented."

The resulting fermentation, the students said, caused a gas explosion in the school cafeteria on the night they left for their class trip.

Silkscreen called his deadly fuel GASP.

"So many dairy cows producing gas left few cows to produce milk," said Shelly. "That combination drove the supply of milk *down* and the price of milk *up*."

Missing Waters Found!

"I was trapped in a silly sinkhole," says Waters

Far from stagnating, Florence Waters spent her months in Sinkiang thinking and inking.

Florence Waters, president of Flowing Waters Fountains, Etc., had a cargo-class ticket to travel on the ill-fated SS *Sinkiang* last September. Fortunately for her, she missed the boat.

While searching for a pair of Sinkiang Blinking Spotted Suckerfish, Waters inhaled an unhealthy dose of the malodorous gases from AIR-igate, Inc. The toxic fumes caused her to faint and fall into a Sinkiang sinkhole.

"Actually, it was more like a *stink*hole," the famous designer said, laughing after her dramatic rescue by friends.

Waters appeared remarkably well despite having spent five months in the sinkhole. She said she survived by eating aquatic weeds and grasses.

"I got the idea by watching the carp," explained Waters, who named her two fish companions Carpe and Diem. "Together, they're *carpe diem*. That's a Latin expression that means 'seize the day.'"

Waters spent the time she was stuck in Sinkiang writing a book she plans to title *Feng Shui: The Art of Flow.* Waters said that when she wasn't working on her book, she "did yoga exercises, made up jokes and told them to myself, and thought a lot about the water shortages in Sinkiang."

The fountain designer mapped out a design for using water from mountain glaciers and rivers to double the amount of usable farmland in Sinkiang.

"I suspect it's how they irrigated farm-land in China before people like Snedley P. Silkscreen started trying to improve on Mother Nature," said Waters.

Waters said she was "not the teeniest bit" afraid that her personal pilot, Ariel Veronica Aytor, and the sixth-grade students from Geyser Creek, Mo., would fail to find her.

"You don't know my friends like I do," said Waters. "There's nothing they can't do once they put their minds—and their noses—to it!"

Endangered Species: A Bunch of Carp

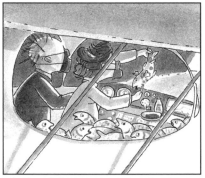

Students' photos capture Sen. Sue Ergass red-handed with Snedley P. Silkscreen, her silent and violent partner.

Experts have confirmed the theory of Geyser Creek Middle School sixth-grade students that the Sinkiang Blinking Spotted Suckerfish is not a rare species at all.

"The kids are right," aquaculturist Marina Byologee said yesterday. "It's just a grass carp painted with red spots."

The Missouri students presented photographs to international authorities that showed U.S. Sen. Sue Ergass applying permanent dyes to grass carp, which she then dropped from an AIR-igate plane piloted by Snedley P. Silkscreen.

"The blinking eyes on the carp reflect the stress the fish experienced after being dropped from such heights, as well as their reaction to the smell of natural gas," biologist Mike Wroskope said.

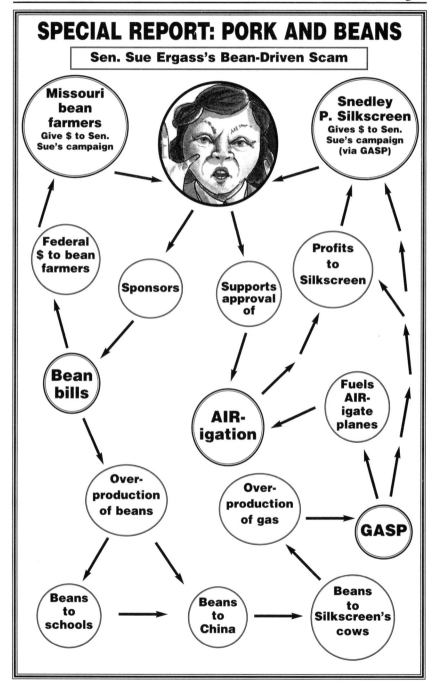

BEAN-MAIL
Brief Educational and/or Administrative Note

To: Mr. Sam N.
Fr: Walter Russ
Re: Mrs. Crabbie
Date: February 23
Time: 2:00 A.M.

If your students want to see Mrs. Crabbie (my mother), they should hurry back. She was admitted to the hospital late last night. It doesn't look good.

I thought the kids might want to thank her-- before it's too late.

★THE GEYSER CREEK GAZETTE★

Our motto: "We have a nose for news!"

Thursday, February 24   **50 cents**

Students Return Home Just in Time to Thank Generous Benefactor

Students say good-bye to Crabbie, who died penniless.

Returning home last night after a whirlwind trip to China during which they rocked international financial markets and rescued a famous fountain designer along with millions of oppressed dairy cows, sixth graders from Geyser Creek Middle School headed straight to the hospital to thank the woman who made their trip possible.

Ima Crabbie never publicly admitted she paid for the students' class trip to China.

"That's just how she was," said Tad Poll, who did chores for Crabbie. "She liked people to think she was a big grouch. But the truth is she was a really nice and generous woman."

The students, who traveled to China late last Friday, took turns telling Crabbie about their recent adventures.

"She wanted to hear every detail, especially about the carp business," said Lily. "She thought that was hilarious. We told her we used our beans and followed our noses, just like she always told us to do."

Sources speculate that Crabbie sold some of

International Markets Rocked

Based on this week's stunning news out of Sinkiang, investors dumped AIR-igate, Inc., stock faster than a sixth grader can dump beans down a sink.

With the rain alternative AIR-igation certain to be discontinued in all countries and Snedley P. Silkscreen, founder and CEO of AIR-igate, Inc., under arrest, it's unlikely that AIR-igate stock can do anything but tank completely. Likewise, bean stocks have gone belly up.

Meanwhile, Rainy-Day Rainwear stocks rebounded on news that rainy days will not be replaced by the rain alternative. In one day Rainy-Day Rainwear stock jumped 12,499,900 percent, from less than one-tenth of one cent per share to $112.50 per share.

her AIR-igate, Inc., stock to finance the students' trip, which, ironically, resulted in the demise of AIR-igate.

"We didn't have the heart to tell her what happened to her AIR-igate stock," said Minnie O.

The woman who made a fortune on AIR-igate stock died penniless just before midnight last night. Her estranged son, Walter Russ, will handle the funeral arrangements.

Wall Street Wrap-up

Stocks to Watch	Yesterday's	Opening price:	Closing price:	Change:
	AIR-igate, Inc.	$320.00	$ .032	-99.99%
	Dyeing to Please	$7.29	$1.82	-75%
	Glum Gum	$ .98	$ .88	-10%
	Rainy-Day Rainwear	$ .0009	$112.50	+12,499,900%
	Tough Beans	$15.24	$2.13	-86%

Cause of Explosion at Middle School Confirmed
"Blame the beans," say feds

Feds say fermented beans caused this scene.

Federal authorities arrived in Geyser Creek yesterday to study the wreckage left by last Friday night's explosion in the middle school cafeteria.

"You can blame the beans for this one," said FBI Agent Frank N. Beens, who confirmed the presence of bean residue in the sink.

The official cause of the explosion was listed as "natural gas resulting from fermented beans in the cafeteria sink and surrounding plumbing, resulting from pork projects related to beans cooked up by the big stinker herself, Sen. Sue Ergass."

FIRST BANK OF GEYSER CREEK
Geyser Creek, Missouri

Juan A. Lone
President

February 24

Mr. Walter Russ
Principal
Geyser Creek Middle School
Geyser Creek, Missouri

Dear Wally,

Please accept my condolences for the loss of your mother. Death is never easy—especially when someone loses her life and her life's fortune at the same time.

I'm especially sorry to have to confront you with a financial matter during this difficult time. But Wally, I made that $100,000 loan to you on Valentine's Day based on my belief that, despite her crabbiness, your mother would leave at least some of her AIR-igate stock to you in her will.

I haven't seen her will, but I've seen the newspaper. AIR-igate stock isn't worth the paper it's printed on. Hence, the $100,000 loan I made you is now dangerously unsecured.

Please contact me immediately so we can discuss this.

Juan A. Lone

Juan A. Lone

GEYSER CREEK MIDDLE SCHOOL
Geyser Creek, Missouri
My new motto: "Mothers are instinctive philosophers."
–Harriet Beecher Stowe

FAX

DATE: February 25
TO: Juan A. Lone
FR: Walter Russ
RE: Explanation

You're right on two counts.

1) In her will, my mother left me her stock in AIR-igate, Inc.

2) That stock is now worthless.

But you seem to have forgotten a third factor: I was one of the few investors left in Rainy-Day Rainwear. My personal 1,000 shares are now worth $112,500. I will repay the $100,000 loan in full later today.

I want to thank you again for approving my loan. At the time, you asked why I needed to borrow the money. I didn't tell you then because I couldn't find the words to explain the situation. Now I'll try.

In her last letter to me, Florence wrote, "I like you." She even called me "a peach." Well, her words caught me off guard. I didn't know how to react. So I gave the letter away. Later I realized that Florence's simple words were the nicest thing anyone had ever said or written to me. That's why I wanted the letter back. Not to frame or hang on my wall. Just to keep in my file cabinet and look at once in a while on a rainy day.

The sixth graders think my mother placed the $100,000 bid that bought the letter. I'd prefer to keep it that way.

Interestingly enough, I have recently acquired something of even greater value that I need to put in a safe place. I'll meet you at the bank at 2:00 P.M. today so that I can repay the loan and put the priceless document in my safe-deposit box.

117

LAST WILL AND TESTAMENT
of
IMOGENE RUSS CRABBIE

I, IMOGENE R. CRABBIE, being of sound mind and sick as a dog, do hereby state my last wishes and . . .

Lookit, it's almost midnight and I don't have the time or energy for fancy lawyer talk. I just want to write a quick note and ask whoever finds this to give it to my son, Walter Russ.

Now, Walter, read this carefully because I'm going to say it only once. Those kids from your school came over to the hospital tonight to thank me for buying that letter from that kooky fountain designer so they could go on their trip.

The kids told me all about their big adventure in China. How it was a dream come true. How they rescued that what's-her-name designer woman.

They went on and on, thanking me and telling me none of it would've been possible without me.

Well, you know as well as I do that I didn't buy that letter. You tried to convince me to bid on it that afternoon you came over to the senior home. I threw you out on your ear. Who would pay $100,000 for a worthless letter?

That's when it dawned on me: YOU would do something stupid like that. You bought that letter, didn't you, Wally? And you must've borrowed money to do it, too, because I know you haven't got squat left after all the money you dumped into Rainy-Day Rainwear.

But you let those kids think I bid on the letter. They thanked me instead of you. Well, Wally, do you know what I think of that? I think you're a pretty good boy. I don't care what anyone says—I'm proud of you.

And because of that—and because I refuse to take orders from a pip-squeak like you—I am NOT LEAVING my money to the kids, as you also asked me to do. I'm leaving everything I have to you. That's right. All my money is yours, including my AIR-igate stock.

Surprised? Well, so am I. I never intended to leave your sorry behind a red dime—until those rugrats started thanking me for something you let them think I did.

You know something else? You were my cutie-patootie first, darn it. (How'd that fountain lady know that's what I used to call you?)

Well, that's all for now, son. Better sign my name and make this official.

Imogene Crabbie February 23
Imogene R. Crabbie
(You can call me MOM.)

P.S. I have a new motto: "Life's a gas!"

WITNESSES

Goldie Fisch 2/23   *Sam N.* February 23
Goldie Fisch   Sam N.

OFFICIAL PROCLAMATION
MAYOR I. B. NEWT

WHEREAS, keeping secrets in a small town like Geyser Creek is impossible,* and

WHEREAS, we all know the Geyser Creek Middle School Sixth-Grade Class was able to travel to Sinkiang, China, to rescue Florence Waters because Wally Russ paid $100,000 for her letter, and

WHEREAS, Wally borrowed $100,000 to buy the letter because of the kind words Florence wrote to him in the letter, and

WHEREAS, Imogene Crabbie left Wally something even more valuable than money (i.e., loving words written to him in her Last Will and Testament), and

WHEREAS, talk may be cheap but a good letter is priceless, and

WHEREAS, nobody ever writes nice letters to me . . .

I hereby proclaim today, MARCH 1, as:

First Annual Write a Nice Letter to Somebody Day!

And I encourage all Geyser Creek residents to take a few minutes out of their busy schedules to write somebody (a friend, a relative, a teacher, and/or a mayor) a letter to tell him/her/them how much you care, and

WHEREAS, store-bought cards are nice and BEAN-mail is convenient, this is something different, folks. I'm talking about an honest-to-goodness LETTER. (And why not add a spritz of your favorite perfume or cologne?)

WHEREAS, requests for alternate designations have been suggested, I hereby proclaim that this day may also be called:

Write a Nice Letter to Your Mother Day!
and/or
Write a Nice Letter to Your Child Day!
and/or
Write a Nice Letter to Your Best Friend Day!
and/or
There's Nothing on Earth Better Than
Writing and/or Reading a Nice Letter
on a Rainy-Day
Day!

---

* Juan A. Lone is my brother-in-law.

March 1

Wally,
Sorry to spill the beans,
but the secret's out.
You're nice!
Shelly and Gil

A Li'l Note
from
Lily and Paddy

Wally: Thanks for being
the BEST princey-pal EVER!

Lily and Paddy

Mr. Russ,
Thanks for being
a great principal!
Tad

My Principal
Dedicated to Wally Russ
By Minnie O.

I don't think I will ever see
a principal as noble as thee;
for who would sacrifice as ye
to giveth so much to me?
So never mind thy petty pedantry;
it's getting pretty clear to me
that you, Wally, are absolutely
principal of the century!

March 1

Dear Sam,

You're my hero.

Very truly yours,

Goldie

P.S. Don't be mad, but Wally never saw your resignation letter. I filed it.

P.P.S. Maybe this is crazy, but I'll take a risk and ask anyway. Would you like to have lunch with me sometime? Bean-free, I promise!

March 1

Goldie,

Of course I want to have lunch with you. How about today?

Sam

P.S. Now I understand what Florence meant. You really *are* priceless, aren't you?

Must get priceless gold for Sam.

GEYSER CREEK MIDDLE SCHOOL
Geyser Creek, Missouri

Sam N.
Sixth-Grade Teacher

My new motto: "To live is so startling it leaves little time for anything else."
—Emily Dickinson

March 1

Principal Russ:

I guess I underestimated you—though your threat of firing me if I took the class to China *did* throw me off the trail. (Of course, if you *hadn't* threatened to fire me, I would've known for sure that something was up.)

Well, what can I say? The bottom line is that I'm proud to know you, sir.

See you at school tomorrow.

Sincerely,

Sam N.

P.S. Hope you'll consider accompanying us on our next class trip.

OFFICIAL SCHOOL MEMO
From the Desk of Principal Walter Russ

My new motto: "Education is what you have left over after you have forgotten everything you've learned." —Anonymous

DATE:	**MARCH 1**
TO:	**ALL STUDENTS AND FACULTY**
FR:	**WALTER RUSS**
RE:	**BACK TO BUSINESS**

Needless to say, these past few weeks have been unusually chaotic and highly irregular.

In order to meet the requirements established by the Missouri Department of Education, ALL students must attend ALL classes for the remainder of the school year. There will be no unexcused absences and no recess. Let's all buckle down and get back to work.

And let's try to keep it quiet, can we?

Thank you.

This is to acknowledge receipt of your cards and letters and to express the fact that... RATS. What I'm trying to say is... JUST thanks. I'm touched. Now get back to your studies.

GEYSER CREEK MIDDLE SCHOOL
SIXTH-GRADE CLASS
Geyser Creek, Missouri
Our NEW class motto: "Carpe carp et carpe diem!"
(Our translation: "Seize the carp and seize the day!")

March 1

Florence Waters
President and Pal
Flowing Waters Fountains, Etc.
Watertown, California

Dear Florence,

This is just a LITTLE letter to say we like you A LOT. Thanks for inspiring us to take the best class trip EVER!

And thanks again for the money tree you sent us last summer. It really worked! We ended up with the most valuable thing in the world: a great friend. (You!)

Going with the Flo in Geyser Creek, Mo.,

Gil   Tad   Lily

Paddy   Shelly   Minnie O.

Florence:
Thanks for helping me see what was right under *my* nose.

Sam N.

P.S. We forgot to ask you something when we saw you in China. What's your motto?*

*A motto is a brief statement expressing a basic principle.

125

'**F**LO**W**ING **W**ATER**S** **F**OUNTAIN**S**, **E**T**C**.'

Watertown, California

March 5

Mr. Sam N.'s Sixth-Grade Class
Geyser Creek Middle School
Geyser Creek, Missouri

Dearest Sixth Graders,

Thank me? Thank *you* for coming to my rescue
in Sinkiang. Isn't it wonderful how the very best
friendships have this natural *sink*ronicity?

Speaking of sinks, with all the excitement in China,
we forgot to discuss yours. Do you still want my
help? You're the sink experts. You found out where
Waters go. But maybe I can schedule a trip to
Geyser Creek and we could collaborate on a design
for your new cafeteria sink. Yes?

And what about some new cafeteria *food*? After all
those beans, wouldn't some pasta hit the spot? I

thought so. Let me work on that.

I don't suppose you'd be interested in one MO'
adventure, would you? Write to me!

I'm so proud to be your friend.

Best regards,

Florence

P.S. to Sam: Keep me posted!

P.P.S. I love mottoes! Must I pick just one? Hmm.
How about: "Make your life your motto!" Wait.
Can a motto describe your basic princi*pal*? If so,
I just thought of one. I'm sending A.V. to deliver
it in person.

✳THE GEYSER CREEK GAZETTE✳

Our motto: "We have a nose for news!"

Friday, March 25   50 cents

Sink Opens! Waters Returns!

Old sink X-stinked and Wally's "not a fink"

Students unveil the Sinkiang-inspired sink designed in collaboration with Florence Waters.

Call it the Sinkiang Sink, because that's what inspired the design of the new sink in the Geyser Creek Middle School cafeteria.

The sink, unveiled yesterday, incorporates many of the natural elements the sixth-grade students observed on their recent class trip to China, including native plant and animal life.

"Of course we don't have any Sinkiang Blinking Spotted Suckerfish in our sink," explained Gil, referring to the phony fish tale he and his classmates reeled in during their trip. "But why shouldn't a cafeteria sink be like a natural basin? We used the Tarim Basin as our model and re-created a mini Sinkiang, China."

The students used the principles of *feng shui* to create a sink that balances the energies of wind and water, and works in harmony with the environment. They collaborated on the sink with renowned designer Florence Waters, who suggested using grass carp as a natural garbage disposal.

"It's a lovely idea," said Waters, who returned to Geyser Creek for the unveiling of the sink. "And it's a nice way to remember the late Mrs. Imogene Crabbie, who the children tell me used carp in a similar way at her home."

Waters and the students had a comfortable budget to work with, thanks to the dramatic rebound of Rainy-Day Rainwear stock. After the rainwear stock split for a fourth time, Geyser Creek Middle School Principal Walter Russ asked the Geyser Creek School Board for permission to cash in the school's 8,000 shares

(Continued on page 2, column 1)

SINK *(Continued from page 1, column 2)*
for $1.2 million. Any money left over from the sink project will be placed in a "rainy-day fund" for unexpected school expenses.

Russ also contributed a $10,000 "rain check" from his personal account to the sink fund.

"Principal Russ was obligated to repay only $500," attorney Barry Cuda said yesterday. "It's clear by his generosity that my client is not a fink. I've spoken with local prosecutors and they've assured me that they have no plans to file charges against Wally for misuse of public funds."

In other news Russ said he has "for the moment" abandoned both his LIMA and BEAN-mail, as well as his goal of creating a letter-free school.

"Until further notice, letters will be permitted on school grounds," Russ said.

In fact it's the campus and school grounds that will occupy much of Russ's attention in the remaining months of the school year.

"The school could use a good general cleaning and the trees on our campus need trimming," Russ said. "The return of federal funding means we can devote attention to where we need it most—our school grounds."

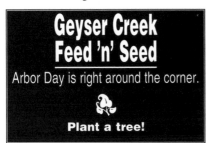

Viva la Lunch!

Italian chef to take over school cafeteria

Chef Angelo will take over school lunch program.

Can the beans! The Geyser Creek Middle School cafeteria is getting a world-class chef.

During yesterday's sink unveiling, designer Florence Waters introduced Chef Angelo, her friend, and told students the Italian chef is moving to Geyser Creek to take over the school lunch program.

Angelo promised students a bean-free menu and said school lunches will rely on family recipes and home-style Italian fare. He will be the first world-class chef ever to cook in Geyser Creek.

"It's about time small-town America got a taste of some *real* cooking," Angelo said.

"I beg your humble pardon," said Angel Fisch, owner of Geyser Creek Cafe.

A lively discussion between Angelo and Angel ensued, until Angelo suggested they collaborate on an evening meal for all who turned out for the sink dedication.

"I have plenty of pasta pots and would be happy to let Angel serve as my assistant," said Angelo.

Angel declined the invitation, saying, "Too many pots spoil the cook."

"Oh dear," said Florence Waters.

Before arriving in Geyser Creek, Waters stopped in Washington, D.C., to ask lawmakers to restore federal funding to schools. She made a special plea for Geyser Creek students and suggested that Congress establish a free gourmet-lunch program for the children to thank them for uncovering the stinky business dealings of AIRigate, Inc., founder and CEO Snedley P. Silkscreen and former U.S. Sen. Sue Ergass.

Ergass and Silkscreen Both Sentenced to 40 Years

Ergass and Silkscreen were convicted on 92 total counts of fraud, graft, corruption, and cruelty to animals, fish, and humans.

(ST. LOUIS) Former U.S. Sen. Sue Ergass and AIR-igate, Inc., founder and CEO Snedley P. Silkscreen were sentenced yesterday to 40 years each by federal judge Rod Enreel, who told the duo: "The ends don't justify the beans."

An AIR-igate plane has been converted into a prison cell for Silkscreen, who will spend his 40-year sentence doing hard labor on a dairy farm, where he'll be guarded by trained attack cows.

Enreel also sentenced Ergass to 40 years of hard labor and an all-bean diet. The former senator will be held in solitary confinement.

"Anything else would constitute cruel and unusual punishment to other prisoners," said the judge, who ordered that all beans from the Beans Lift America's Spirit Tremendously! (BLAST!) drive be delivered to the prison cafeteria to be used in preparing Ergass's meals.

Earlier this month Ergass was impeached and convicted by her former colleagues in Congress, who also voted to remove bean soup from the Senate dining room menu.

Dear Inmate Sue

Editor's note: As part of her sentence, former Sen. Sue Ergass will answer actual questions from her former constituents.

Dear Inmate Sue:
Prisons have very strong *yin* energy. Have you considered planting trees and growing flowers to add *yang*? Or you could add such *yang* elements as boulders, pebbles, or stones to your garden.
Minnie O., Geyser Creek, MO

Dear Minnie:
I have a boulder tied around my foot. Does that count?
Inmate Sue

Dear Inmate Sue:
How are you enjoying the food in prison?
Angel, Geyser Creek, MO

Dear Angel:
Ha ha. Very funny.
Inmate Sue

Dear Former Senator Sue:
What's your motto?
Tad Poll, Geyser Creek, MO

Dear Tad Poll:
I have two mottoes:
"Never eat more than you can lift."
—Miss Piggy
"If you want a friend in Washington, get a dog." —Harry Truman

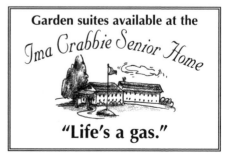

Wall Street Wrap-up

Stocks to Watch	Yesterday's	Opening price:	Closing price:	Change:
	AIR-igate, Inc.	*no longer trading*	--	--
	Dyeing to Please	$ .87	$ .57	-34%
	Glum Gum	$ .57	$ .42	-26%
	Rainy-Day Rainwear	$155.00	$170.50	+10%
	Tough Beans	$ .90	$ .45	-50%

Got Milk!

Principal Wally Russ has a cow when he meets school's new herd.

Designer Florence Waters surprised locals by arriving in town with a small herd of cows transported by private plane from China to Geyser Creek.

"The students and I worked closely with Chinese authorities to free the AIR-igate cows so they could graze on the now naturally irrigated pastures," said Waters. "But after the children left, I sensed that some of the cows missed them and wanted to show their appreciation. What better way for the animals to say thank you than by providing fresh milk for milk shakes in the school cafeteria?"

Waters also brought a dairy cow for Geyser Creek Cafe.

PUBLIC NOTICE

Geyser Creek Middle School is now accepting bids for a major tree-trimming and pruning project. Contact principal Walter Russ for all inquiries regarding the trees.

Mr. Russ:

Do you think Florence would consider bidding on this?

Should we ask her?

Sam N.

Yes and (sigh) yes. (WR)

COMING SOON!

From the waterlogged sisters who brought you *Regarding the Fountain* and *Regarding the Sink* comes:

Regarding the Trees: A Splintered Saga Rooted in Secrets

(Because sometimes you need to branch out a little.)

Read on for a sneak peek. . . .

GEYSER CREEK MIDDLE SCHOOL
Geyser Creek, Missouri
Our NEW school motto: *Go with the Flo*

Mr. Walter Russ
Principal

April 1

Ms. Florence Waters
President
Flowing Waters Fountains, Etc.
Watertown, California

Dear Ms. Waters,

As you might have noticed on your recent visit to Geyser Creek, the trees on our school campus have become quite overgrown. One tree in particular, a giant weeping willow behind the school, is in need of serious pruning, if not total elimination. The remaining 100 or so trees require trimming.

I can't imagine you have the experience, expertise, or necessary equipment for a tree-trimming project of this magnitude. Then again, I've learned better than to assume anything when it comes to you, Ms. Waters. If you would like to bid on this tree-trimming and pruning job, please advise soonest.

As part of my yearly evaluation by the Society of Professional Administrators, I will be graded on the appearance of our school campus, as well as on how I award and administer contracts for projects such as this.

In the past, evaluators have reviewed correspondence between administrators (me) and contractors (you) to judge the relationship and to look for lapses in professionalism or ethical conduct. This need not be a concern for you, but it might explain the rather direct nature of my correspondence as we proceed with this project.

The evaluators will be here in early June, so time is of the essence. For this reason I must be very clear with you about my intentions regarding the trees and my relationship with you. In short: **I need a proposal from you.**

If you'd prefer to give me a call and state your proposal over the phone, that would be acceptable, too. **Just give me a ring.**

Sincerely,

Walter

Walter Russ

P.S. I'm a little concerned about your friend Chef Angelo and his plans for our school lunch program.

One of the goals of feng shui is to maximize the beneficial movement of chi, the universal life force present in all things, through an environment.

Chi nourishes our lives when it meanders like a graceful river. But when the flow of chi is blocked, it becomes stale and stagnant, like a weed-choked pond or a clogged sink.